With All My Heart

Based on True Events

ELIZABETH MCLENNAN

authorHOUSE®

AuthorHouse™ LLC
1663 Liberty Drive
Bloomington, IN 47403
www.authorhouse.com
Phone: 1-800-839-8640

© 2014 Elizabeth McLennan. All rights reserved.

Book cover design by Lauren Quintal

No part of this book may be reproduced, stored in a retrieval system, or
transmitted by any means without the written permission of the author.

Published by AuthorHouse   09/25/2014

ISBN: 978-1-4969-1366-1 (sc)
ISBN: 978-1-4969-1362-3 (e)

Library of Congress Control Number: 2014909093

Any people depicted in stock imagery provided by Thinkstock are models,
and such images are being used for illustrative purposes only.
Certain stock imagery © Thinkstock.

This book is printed on acid-free paper.

Because of the dynamic nature of the Internet, any web addresses or links contained in
this book may have changed since publication and may no longer be valid. The views
expressed in this work are solely those of the author and do not necessarily reflect the
views of the publisher, and the publisher hereby disclaims any responsibility for them.

Dedicated To
Emilia Taraby Zakaib

For My Family
My husband Steve,
My daughters Lauren and Chelsea
My stepkids Tyler and Cassandra
My nieces Ashley and Melanie

Praise for With All My Heart

With All My Heart is a must read!! The author clearly speaks "with all her heart"; her truth is inspirational! She speaks to others who have also lived many challenges and traumatic experiences, and encourages forgiveness and love to find true happiness! A must read for anyone, but especially those struggling!

- Karen Gurr

With All My Heart is a life story well told and bound to inspire anyone who has endured a difficult childhood. Heartbreaking but ultimately empowering, the book's healing message is that no one need be a victim of their childhood.

- Cheryl Cornacchia

With All My Heart was so Inspirational!! How one person turns such negativity into such strength and positivity. I enjoyed the book immensely. It took me one day to read and I could not put it down!

- Veronica Dluhosh

A sincere story about overcoming some of life's most difficult challenges. Genuinely written from the heart. Keep a tissue handy!

- Michelle Wesley

With All My Heart is an awe-inspiring story about courage and survival. From a very young age, the author faces heart-wrenching losses and challenges, that anyone would have a hard time surviving. She not only survives but makes it through with an undying spirit and determination. This book is an inspiration to every person struggling to work through the pains and neglect of their childhood. Through her struggles there are triumphs, proving that each individual has the ability and the power to become the author of the rest of their lives.

- Paola Samuel

With All My Heart was an easy, honest read...DEEP from her soul... heartbreaking and heartwarming...what a relief it must be for Beth and so enlightening to her family and friends. A treasure to keep.

-Renda Lasdin

The author exposes the naked truth of her stolen childhood, and life thereafter through her words in *With All My Heart*. She clearly wanted the world to see how this does not define who you are and show people what inner strength can look like. We all have it in us... sometimes it's just buried a little deeper.

-Marie Hudon

Such a special book told with such sincerity and honesty. Giving others hope that no matter what ones past experiences may be, whether good or bad, every experience contributes to the person they are today. It is what they do with their experiences, what attitude they chose to posses that will decide their future outcomes.

-Carol Renshaw

I found *With All My Heart* to be so interesting. It made me laugh and made me cry. With all the ups and downs Elizabeth faced, she still came out shining. I admire her strength and patience but what I admire the most is that she never gave up. I have so much respect for the author.

- Lynn Hendy

Heartwarming and touching! The author opens her heart to the world in hopes of making a difference in someone's life; and I am sure she has.

- Katherine Debs

So many of us at some point or another, feel that life can seem hopeless with no chance of change. This book proves us wrong and helps us see that we can all turn our lives around. Our thoughts and positive outlook will change the course of our lives!

-Rita Katchouni

An inspiring story of the human spirit. No one can take the fire out of your soul and the passion in your heart.

-Norma Issa

A great fast read. The author shows courage in trusting her authentic self and teaches us, that with determination we can overcome whatever is thrown our way.

-Linda Renshaw

What an inspiring life. And I can only imagine how she felt after she wrote it. I think I will be writing some letters to move on and forgive. You don't even know how it helped me...it reads like a journal and I really never felt bad for her. I feel like I can do that! It also brought up some memories and things that I have been in denial about. I actually called my sister and asked some very big questions. We spoke about things we had never talked about. Made things about our childhood almost come to a close, now that we both know it actually happened.

-P.C.

Thank You For Inspiring Me

Inspirational people and environments allows for creativity to manifest into so many great things. Without inspiration those creative juices can lie stagnant. I feel so blessed to have so many amazing people who are in my life. Although my hopes and dreams involve inspiring others, many people have and continue to inspire and help me in so many ways. To my amazing family and friends who support me everyday – you know who you are and I hope you feel the love! Thank you from the bottom and *With All My Heart*.

Contents

Prologue

My name is Elizabeth Mary McLennan, but my friends call me Beth. I began my journey of writing this book by following my heart and pushing away fear. I have felt compelled to share personal experiences in hopes to give a voice to those who feel they can't speak. I have always lived my life trying to help others in some way. I have also wanted to inspire others to overcome obstacles and make choices that will allow them to feel more in control of their own life.

Over the years, many friends have told me to write a book about my life. I never saw my story as anything anyone would be interested in reading. Although I did not have the easiest childhood, I always felt that things could have been worse. They definitely could have been; turn on the news, listen to people's stories, everyone has overcome challenges and difficulties.

There have been many times in my life when I have felt very alone or almost unable to cope. I always knew that I had the choice to be miserable or happy. Although it didn't happen over night, I chose to find ways to be happy. I have evolved from a negative, angry teen and young adult, into a positive, empowered, and happy woman.

I feel that everyone has been put on this earth to live a specific journey in his or her lifetime. Sometimes life's journey may be difficult or painful, which may be out of your control. Living certain experiences and learning through mistakes is part of your evolution. I have a blessed life, and even though it did not always feel that way, I know the experiences were meant to teach me lessons and give me strength. I no longer fear what may happen, because I am confident that I can handle anything. Life is filled with amazing experiences as well as challenges, but the important thing is how you learn to cope.

I look at life as though I am driving along a highway going towards my destination. There will be many hours of peaceful driving and beautiful scenery. There may also be curves, bumps, and detours along this highway. Some detours may take longer than others. There are often tragedies, injured people, freak accidents, and even deaths. This is what our journey in life is like. The only choice we have is how we handle experiences that come into our path. Would you ever just stop along the highway and decide to not move forward? Believe in your inner strength, in your own power and ability to overcome obstacles and achieve anything you want.

Childhood has a huge impact on your life, but it does not have to define you. It is important for those who have been through more difficulties to allow that inner child to feel happy and safe. Some of you may look back on your childhood and feel pure happiness, while others may not. As children, we don't have the same level of control over certain experiences. As adults we can make better choices and decide who we want to be.

Dreams really do come true: make them happen! Have belief in yourself, faith in The Universe and in the process of life. Hold on to the belief that you have the power to heal, and that you deserve to live the life that you have always dreamed of living.

My hope is that you will feel empowered to help yourself heal from the past, live a better life, and make choices to improve yourself every day. If I can do it, you can too. We all have the power. I hope *With All My Heart* that my story helps and inspires you in many ways.

With All My Heart,
Beth

"Faith is taking the first step even when you don't see the whole staircase." Martin Luther King Jr.

The Serenity Prayer

GOD please grant me

The **SERENITY** *to accept the
things I cannot change*

The **COURAGE** *to change
the things I can,*

The **WISDOM** *to know the difference*

Changed Forever: 2001

THERE WERE MANY TRAUMATIC EVENTS, which took place in my childhood, but I lived my life saying they were "no big deal". Mimi used to say: "nothing is a big deal to you, is it"? That was how I felt. Then, something that had been buried so deep, unveiled itself.

There was always an underlying anger inside me, which I could not explain. It was a deep unhappiness and heaviness. All the therapy in the world couldn't ease that feeling. I went to many different psychologists who all felt I had handled my childhood well; I thought so too. Except for that one thing that was fighting and screaming to come out. I could feel it but I could not explain it. In my mid thirties, the one thing that changed my life in so many ways finally erupted out of me like a volcano. I guess The Universe felt I was ready to handle it.

The memory first came to me in a nightmare. Then, in my waking moments, as I said the words "my father sexually abused me" my whole world began to spin. I could not breathe. The heaviness on my chest was absolutely unbearable. Everything came flooding back; all the times my father either came into my room, or later in years reached out to touch my leg. There were times when the smell of him made me feel sick, unknowingly angry, it was all too much. I broke down like I had never broken down before. I cried like I had never cried before. It didn't take long before the shock set in. It was then that I became totally detached, only to keep from bursting into tears. I could feel myself slipping into a dark space. I knew I couldn't lose it now; I had to keep it together because my daughters needed me. I had to be strong and get through this.

A new healing journey began. There was so much anger, so much sadness. I didn't want any of it. I felt disillusioned. I felt like someone must feel after they had been raped. How can I share this? My father had been dead for years and everyone thought he was the greatest man. I couldn't talk to or share this with anyone. I felt ashamed. I was scared. My mind was spinning, and for one of the first times in my life I felt out of control.

There was only one person I could speak to, Mimi. I was scared, because I didn't want to worry or upset her. But I had no choice, she was the only link I had to my past, the only person who could answer questions. Mimi loved me unconditionally, and therefore wouldn't judge me. For a brief moment, after I had voiced the truth, Mimi's eyes gazed deeply into mine. Then she began to share some things my Mom told her, things that she never told anyone.

As time went on, through hypnotherapy, psychotherapy, and energetic healing therapies, I realized that I had to let this go. I've accepted that it will always be a part of me; there will always be moments where the memories come flooding back, a scene in a movie, or a nightmare out of the blue. But I had to let go. As part of this process it was recommended that I write a letter to my dad, so I did:

Dear Dad,

I hate you. I hate everything you did to me. I hate the childhood I had. I hate that you did not protect me. I hate that you were someone to fear instead of someone keeping me safe.

I hated your smell and never knew why. I remember feeling guilty that I hated it so much. I hated when you would reach over in the car and touch my leg. I always remember pulling away. You always made a comment. You knew. You knew what you did. What you did to me was sick, it was wrong, and it changed me. I have lived, searching for answers, wanting to be a better person, and trying to understand some of my choices. I always felt like I was such a bad person for certain choices I made.

After you died, I cried for a few minutes and then stopped and I felt nothing. My big sister Monica even asked me why I stopped crying. I said it was because I was fine, but I had no idea why I shut down so suddenly. I felt as though I had to be sad. At times I would cry, but I wasn't sure if it was because others around me were sad, or because you were dead. All I really felt was indifferent. At your funeral everyone talked about what a great guy you were, I know to some, you were. I was told that you knew I resented you. Did you tell anyone why? It was awful to hear that, and at the time I did not understand. Now I do, and you were right, I did resent you for so many reasons, and still do.

I have spent months and months trying to make sense of this, trying to understand how a father could do this. The only person I trusted to share this with, was Mimi. She told me how you would come home drunk, go to mom and she would kick you out. She was miserable with you. I guess that was why you came to me. My bedroom was right across the hall. What you didn't get from mom, you got from your very young daughter. How sad, how sad for me. So yes, I hate you for it. I have had so many screwed up relationships, and therefore have carried so much guilt wondering why and how I could have made some of the choices I made. I guess what you did to me; you didn't do when you were sober. I know you were a lost man…

As I was writing the letter, I was crying and I didn't even notice. The tears where streaming down my cheeks. I screamed and yelled at him. I hated how I was feeling; I hated the anger, and I hated the hate. I decided in order for me to heal as best I could, I had one thing left to do. I knew how I had to end my letter.

...Dad, I am choosing to forgive you. Although I am not sure if I can stop hating you, I do not want to live with anger anymore. I can only learn to resolve my own pain. I understand that you were so unhappy, that maybe you did not even known what you were doing. Or at least I want to try to believe that. I am choosing to let go, and try my best to accept my sadness when it comes, and heal as best I can. I thank you for giving me life, and I am choosing to forgive you. I will never forget, but I will not let this control my life.

I hope you are more at peace dead than you were alive.

Your daughter,
Elizabeth

It has taken me years and years to try to heal from this. Can anyone truly heal from something like sexual abuse? There is, and always will be, residue from this. It is something that stays with me, but I push it away as best I can.

Once I had written the letter, I had a very strange sense of relief. This helped me make sense of some of the other demons, the bad choices I made. It helped me to understand who I was as a person. It was almost like finding a missing piece of a puzzle. That feeling gnawing at me, like something trapped trying to escape, had now dissipated.

Some feel I may need to deal with this on a deeper level. Personally, I don't see the point. Why keep rehashing the past? I definitely don't want to keep reliving this experience, although it comes up without warning from time to time. I can't change what happened, and so I prefer to leave it in the past as much as humanly possible. As I continue to grow and evolve as a person, residue from this experience haunts me. It lies dormant, then without any warning, I find myself gasping for air. As my heart begins to race, I can feel the tightening in my chest and the emotions begging to burst through me. My conscious mind, knows that I am reacting on a deeper level. As hard as I try to be logical, the cellular memory of the past experience is too powerful for me to ignore. The emotions rise through my gut, and into my throat. As my emotions continue to erupt, I begin to feel powerless. As I try to talk myself into a state of peace and calm, I visualize myself as the small child I once was. I close my eyes and picture myself as that child that I must now protect and I allow the surge of emotion to release. I focus on releasing these overwhelming emotions as I hold her in my arms, reminding myself that I am now safe. I am a survivor, and I use that strength to give rise to my fighter instincts, which have become a vital part of my survival.

I survived. What I realized later on in life is how I survived. In order to survive such a traumatic event at such a young age, it was as though I left my own body, I was completely detached. The shocking moments in my childhood are the most prominent memories I have.

I will always be grateful to my dad for giving me life. Over the years I have come to realize how sad his life must have been. He was orphaned and maybe he was abused as well. He grew up with his aunts, three brothers, and one sister. They all had it rough but it didn't give him the right to abuse me. I also feel as though it was bigger than him. He was always drunk when it happened, which I guess was my reason for forgiving him.

I did not share this story to shock people or make my dad seem like a horrible person. I want to keep some good memories of him; after all he was my dad. Maybe I am too forgiving, but this is who I am, I believe in forgiveness. I believe it is the only way for me to heal and move forward. Life is about learning how to heal from past experiences and become more empowered. I have shared this to help others, because I know I am not alone, and that many people have been abused.

The Beginning: 1964-1973

From the moment I was born, my godmother Mimi was by my side. She was my mom's best friend, not a blood relative, and yet we were closer than family. Her real name was Emilie but my sister Monica, who was born five years before me, named her Mimi. Mimi had really wanted to be the godmother to my sister, but my mom asked her sister-in-law, our aunt Ginny. My mom promised Mimi she could be godmother to her second child. It was difficult for my mom to get pregnant again, but some things are just meant to be. I was meant to be.

It was mid December 1964 while my mom was at the hairdresser when the pain pierced through her. I was not due until mid January, so this was scary for her. I was born December 16th, 1964, in Montreal, Canada, one month premature. I was in a hurry and have been ever since; at least that's what Mimi always said. My parents were both born in Canada, but my paternal grandparents were born in Syria. They had died when my dad was young so I never knew them, nor did I ever hear stories about them. My maternal grandparents were born in Scotland, and they'd been divorced by the time I was born. I don't have much memory of them either.

I was in an incubator for over a week. I never thought much about that, until I had kids. Babies need to be held! Nonetheless I must have felt the love from my mom and Mimi, who would come to the hospital every day. My mom was scared of me because I was so small, so Mimi was with me a lot. From the moment I was born there was an unexplainable connection and bond between Mimi and me. She was my guardian, my Angel, then and now. She always will be.

At about two and a half years old, I had to have eye surgery. I was a cross-eyed little thing, but lucky for me the surgery to cut the muscle made my eye straight again. Mimi told me that when I woke up from surgery, I was strapped to the bed, so I wouldn't touch my eye. It broke her heart and even though both she and my mom were there when I woke up, I whimpered, opened my one good eye, and asked for Mimi. I had a patch on my left eye for a few weeks. Mimi loved telling me stories of how I would still want to do everything for myself. I would pull up a chair, and climb on the counter to get myself a glass or a plate. As she always said, I was little miss independent.

I remember stories of how I would swim in our pool every day, and how my little dog Bobbie used to chase me around our dining room table biting my diaper. I am not sure at which point we didn't have him anymore, but afterward we had another dog, a terrier that I named Missy. This was a perfect name for a dog that always had "accidents" right next to the newspaper we laid out for him. He would literally just miss the paper.

I was about four or five years old when we moved into a bigger home, but it didn't have a swimming pool. I remember making new friends, playing in the street, and walking over to the school by myself to hit tennis balls against the wall. I was still independent and continued to spend much of my time amusing myself. I remember being shy even with my own mom, or at least that is how I always described it, but looking back I am not sure if shy is the right word. I can remember waking up some mornings and not being able to even say good morning or look at my mom, which only made sense, as I grew older. The truth of my years in this home had been buried so deep.

One Halloween, my dog Missy took off out of the front door. I chased after her, but she was nowhere to be found. I was heart-broken. We went to the dog shelter to see if Missy would turn up. On our very first visit, there was the most adorable dog that was a mix of a beagle and terrier. Every time I went near her cage, she whimpered, so I stopped to pet her and she wagged her tail like crazy. I was a total traitor, because now all I wanted to do was to take this dog home. Of course my mom said no, wanting to find Missy. I wanted this other dog so badly, even though I felt bad about Missy being gone. Other people walked by the cage and the dog did not react. I walked by, and it was as though she was talking to me. Needless to say I cried all the way home. A week passed, and we had gone back to the shelter. Finally, the day came. We rescued the new dog and I was the happiest kid on the planet. After much thought, my mom, my sister, and I named the dog Gigi. I adored Gigi and she adored me. I took her for walks and cuddled with her. She was my best friend.

My mom was not a very happy woman. People described her as a beautiful woman. She was very tall, about 5' 10". I can remember her long feet because she would ask me to tickle them while we watched The Pig and Whistle, Sonny and Cher, or The Carol Burnett Show. Her marriage to my dad was not a match made in heaven. He had other women, he drank too much, and he gambled. He would come home drunk and she would send him away. When I was old enough and when I had questions, Mimi shared the stories that she had never told anyone.

Many years before my sister and I were born, my mother lost her only sibling, her brother whom she loved and adored. It was not just the fact that he died; it was also the way he died. He was having a seizure on the street and the cops picked him up thinking he was on drugs, so they tossed him in jail, where he died over night. Mimi told me that my mom never got over this tragedy.

One night late in the evening the doorbell rang. I was the one who answered it with my mom. I remember this because I was scared. There were two men in suits, wearing hats, and flashing their badges at us. They wanted to search our home, and I had no idea what was going on. My mom was terrified so she called my dad right away. All I know is that before my dad got home, these men were going through every drawer, tossing things, and scaring us. My dad eventually arrived and I don't know what he did or didn't do, but the men finally left. I was still scared, not feeling any comfort from my dad.

I do remember fun stuff too, though. Driving up north in our station wagon, with my mom, Mimi, Aunt Betty and Uncle Ernest. We would sing songs, like "Take Me Out to the Ball Game", and yell the last line and then the adults would cackle away. While we were all up north the adults would drink and get pretty funny. I even remember the one time Mimi fell asleep under the dining room table!

Years passed and the next memory I have is the summer of 1973, when I was eight years old. I was up in our country home for two weeks alone with my mom, who lay on the couch and drank. She didn't scare me, but at eight years old I was left to take care of myself. My mom just lay on the couch drinking and sleeping. She had told me she was proud of me for taking care of myself, and that when she got better, she would buy me a watch. To this day, a watch holds a special place in my heart, especially one I receive as a gift. I always feel that in some way it is from my mom.

When Mimi and I used to talk about that summer, she said that by the time she came up north a few weeks later, my hair was in huge knots and I probably had not showered in weeks. My nickname was green teeth, so chances are I never brushed my teeth either. Mimi also said that every pot, dish, and can of Chef Boy-Ar-Dee was on the counter. I fed myself for those few weeks, and I am sure as most kids would at that age, I fed myself junk and more junk.

What nobody knew, especially not Mimi was that I swam in our lake by myself every day. Not just a little swim either, I was going across the lake, canoeing by myself, snorkeling, going to a little beach nearby, and all without a life jacket.

By the end of August, my dad and sister showed up with a family friend who was a doctor. The decision was made to hospitalize my mom. My sister was going to live with our aunt and uncle, and I was going to live with Mimi. I remember sitting in the back seat of the car, not really knowing what was going on. I was feeling guilty because I was so excited to be going to live with Mimi, but I knew my mom was sick. I heard my dad tell my sister that my mom had a 50/50 chance. I had no clue what that meant. When I asked, I was told that she was going to get better.

I began grade three living with Mimi, and her daughter Helen. Mimi did not grow up with much; in fact she grew up in an orphanage. As of twelve years of age Mimi worked in a factory, and always had to work hard for every penny she made. She struggled her whole life and things were not easy. She'd had no choice but to kick her husband out once she discovered that he had a girlfriend, leaving her as a single mom to raise her four kids on her own. Shirley, David, Helen, and Peter shared their mom with me. Mimi had paid her dues and yet still took me into her home with an open heart. Even Peter's girlfriend Joy helped me with my bird project, and took me out for ice cream, or to the amusement park. They all showered me with the love and attention I needed. Mimi was still working and had no idea how she could handle her work, home, and now me. Nonetheless she did it, and did it with such love.

My father brought me to Mimi's with my suitcase. He didn't even come in; he just dropped me off like a piece of luggage. Mimi enrolled me in my new school for grade three. The school was right around the corner, and every morning Mimi and Helen would watch me cross the street and then we would wave goodbye to each other. I was given a key around my neck so I wouldn't lose it, and every day I walked home to a lunch Mimi left for me in the fridge. The T.V. tray was set up in front of the television and I always watched The Flintstones, while eating my egg salad sandwich, green olives, and chips. YUM!

I didn't really understand what was going on. I knew my mom was sick and I remember going to the hospital once. Mimi had to sneak me in, because kids were not permitted in the rooms. Thinking back, I realized that once again this was a time when I was shy with my mom and couldn't say much. Mimi also told me this, and she remembered having to tell me to give my mom a hug.

I was forced to do three things when I moved in with Mimi; go to Sunday school, continue to take accordion lessons, and take ballet lessons after school. Sunday school was traumatic for a shy kid like me. Actually "shy" might be the wrong word, more like mute. I had the hardest time looking at anyone or saying hello. I don't remember being in church before this Sunday school experience. I literally shook in my pants throughout each class. If I was ever asked a question, I felt like I was going to die. So finally, Mimi, seeing the anxiety I was going through, let me off the hook. Then there were the much-dreaded accordion lessons, but they too, ended quickly.

For the first two weeks of school I would come home at the end of the day with a stomach ache. Mimi thought I was sad about my mom, although I was, that was not my problem. My problem was this girl Josie. She was a tough kid and was giving me a hard time. The reason ballet classes after school were not fun, was because Josie decided I would be a great candidate to pick on. So every day, walking into ballet, different things would happen. I would get whacked on the head with the ballet shoebox, be given a little shove to be laughed at, or have a door slammed in my face. Whatever she could do to bug me, she would do. And she laughed cause I was so little. While this felt like an eternity, this only took place over a two week period. When I finally told Mimi and Helen what was going on, Helen flipped out! She came to my rescue and what she did the following day, changed everything. I was walking out of school, knowing Helen was waiting in her car. Of course this one day Josie was ignoring me. I knew I could get a reaction if I let the door close in her face, so I did. It really peeved her off, so she shoved me hard enough that I went falling forward. Helen saw this, and as Josie came to cross the street in front of her car, Helen stepped on the gas and then slammed on the breaks about an inch away from Josie. The poor girl went white. But that wasn't enough. Helen got out and yelled at her saying, "if you ever "Fu$%^&" go near her again I will "Fu$%^&" come back and break both your "Fu$%^&" legs!!" Wooooooo..... Josie shook in her pants and ran off. I was terrified, but pretty pleased all at the same time. Helen had a temper, and in this case I was so very happy to have her on my side, which she has been my whole life.

The very next day, on September 13th, 1973 after school Josie invited me to her house. I was so happy, but maybe just a tad scared. Maybe this was pay back for the "wrath" of Helen. First we had to stop at Mimi's to ask permission. I walked up the stairs and I heard the phone ringing. I heard Mimi on the phone saying, "oh ok, do you want me to come to the hospital?" I asked if everything was okay, she said yes, and off I went to Josie's house. We had a fun time together. Her sister ended up marrying my cousin, so it was a good thing we became friends.

Why did I remember the exact date of my new friend inviting me to her house? That night all of Mimi's kids were over for dinner. After we finished eating everyone went quiet. Mimi asked me to sit on her lap. She gave me a hug with tears in her eyes. Mimi spoke softly, "honey, your mommy loved you very much, but she went to Jesus". My thought was, *not him again.* I should have listened in Sunday school because I really was not sure what she was trying to tell me. Maybe I just didn't want to believe what she was telling me. I looked around the table and when I saw everyone crying, I knew my mom died. I jumped off Mimi's lap, and ran to the bathroom. I can still picture the pink tiles on the walls with the black border. I remember sitting on the toilet, realizing that I didn't even have to pee. I sat there wondering if I would ever see my mom again.

Then the nightmares began, and they were always the same. I would be walking into the restaurant at the shopping center. My mom used to take my sister and me there for lunch, and we always sat in these big oval booths. I would be frantically walking through the shopping center, always by myself, knowing I was looking for my mom. When I arrived at the restaurant, she was sitting in the booth smiling. I was always so excited, feeling so happy, thinking, *I knew it, she is still alive.* But as I got closer, my mom got further and further away, until she disappeared. I would wake up with that heaviness and sadness, realizing all over again, that my mom was gone forever. I would never see her again.

Recently my daughter Sydney asked me to watch the movie "Beaches", with Barbara Hershey and Bette Midler. I was shocked at the impact it had on me. For those who have never seen it, it is a story of friendship and loss. The story could have been about Mimi, my mother, and me. What struck me to the core, was this little girl, how much she wanted to see her mother, and how sad she was when her mother died. I don't remember asking to see my mom while she was in the hospital, nor do I remember dealing with her death.

My dad didn't let me go to my mom's funeral. During one of many therapy sessions in my thirties, I realized that because of this I never had closure. Attending the funeral would have given me the chance to grieve properly, and say goodbye. This important step was missing so I always lived in this fantasy world that maybe one day, my mom would come back. Maybe she was hiding out. She was gone forever and nobody really talked about her to me, except for Mimi in later years.

Only when I was much older did Mimi tell me different stories about when my mom died and how I reacted. I have no memory of certain things, things that would've had a huge impact on me. Mimi told me how I would sit on her bed for hours and just stare into space. She would wave her hand in front of my face and I would not respond. I did this for months and months, always playing silently by myself, as if in my own world. She took me to a doctor who said it was normal, that it was from the shock of losing my mom at such a young age. Mimi shared stories about our time together and how much she wanted to keep me with her forever. If only she had.

We used to spend time with Mimi's daughter Shirley, and son-in-law Theodore. Shirley remembers how, at that time, I never spoke. I would spend an entire weekend never uttering one word. I looked happy because I was with Mimi. I amused myself by diving in and out of the pool collecting change they would throw in for me to get. In years that followed, I spent many weekends with Mimi, Helen, Shirley, and Theodore, in the country, and I cherish all of those happy memories.

As grade three was coming to an end, my father wanted me to go to our home up north to meet his new girlfriend. I was not happy about that, at all.

Meeting Priscilla was not a fun experience. She looked frazzled, and was drunk the ENTIRE weekend! She staggered around and didn't make much sense to me. Whatever, I was going back to Mimi's.

A month later, I was graced with another visit from my father. He asked me to sit down next to him, something I never wanted to do. He proceeded to tell me that he and Priscilla were getting married. I put my index finger in my mouth, pressed it into my cheek to make that popping sound, and said "whoopie" in the most sarcastic voice I could muster. I then ran to the bathroom and locked the door, refusing to come out until he left. Once Mimi reassured me he had gone, I slowly opened the door and then ran into her arms and cried.

Unfortunately, my dad returned one dreadful day at the end of August. Mimi held me in her arms and began to cry. I was numb, and did not shed a tear. I got into the car feeling awful. I looked out of the rear window, waving to Mimi as she got farther away. I was nine years old, scared, and leaving Mimi to go live in an apartment with my father and "mommy dearest". More than anything, I wanted to stay with Mimi.

The Alcoholic Stepmother: 1974

THE ADVENTURE BEGAN, WE MOVED three times within ten months. I was so fortunate to meet some great friends. Leigh was one my friends, and one of my angels. Her family saved me many times, opening their home to me. I loved being at school and hated when the bell rang at the end of the day, my stomach would churn. I always had this dreaded sense of fear, emptiness, and sadness. There was a huge void inside me, which I could ignore while I was at school with friends, but the minute I was walking home alone, that awful feeling would come back.

Priscilla was only twenty-five years old, and my dad was fifty. I remember people talking about that. If she hadn't scared me so much, I probably wouldn't have cared about her age. She was an attractive woman. Tall, and slim, with long blonde hair that she always wore piled on the top of her head. She always seemed to wear bright lipstick, smeared around her mouth. For those who have seen the movie "American Hustle", Priscilla looked very similar to the character played by Jennifer Lawrence.

The first thing on Priscilla's list was to get rid of my sister. I was devastated. How could they do this? Looking back Monica was the lucky one, although she didn't feel so luck at the time. I will never forget my sister lifting me up onto the counter in the bathroom. Monica looked at me, and then told me that she was going to boarding school with her friend. I cried so hard, and the pain was so intense I could barely breath. I felt sick to my stomach. Every time she came home for a weekend I was so excited. Then when she had to leave again, that sickening feeling in the pit of my stomach would come back. I needed my big sister, and my dad was ruining that too. I hated him.

With Priscilla, there was always a daily adventure. I either came home to Priscilla passed out, staggering around, yelling about something, crying, or throwing things. You name it she did it. Then there were times when she was nowhere to be found, but there would be blood all over the floor, or jam on the ceiling. Seriously, how does someone get jam on a ceiling? I guess when you're drunk as a skunk anything is possible. I came to realize that we probably got kicked out of the apartments due to her destructive behavior.

I lived through grade four, in constant fear, and I mean constant. At night there was always some kind of screaming, yelling, and crying, usually ending with my father smacking Priscilla, which was never a good sound to hear. I would literally be shaking in my bed, and knowing my dad was going to come into my room, made me even more scared. I had no idea why it scared me so much but it did. With my heart beating out of my chest, I would hold the blankets so high up around my neck hoping my bedroom door wouldn't open. I would feel as though I couldn't move. I didn't want to move, and I would pretend I was fast asleep. There was nothing that I wanted more than to go back to live with Mimi. Somehow morning would come, and as hard as I tried, I couldn't remember what happened after the screaming.

One of the many loud nights, along with the screaming, and yelling I heard a huge crash; I was terrified. I wasn't sure if I blacked out from fear, but the next thing I knew it was morning. I cautiously walked out of my room, stepping on a giant piece of glass in the hall. The pain pierced through my foot and when I looked down I noticed blood all over the floor. At first I panicked thinking it was from my foot, but then

I noticed glass and blood all through the hallway and around the corner to where this glass table had been. I had to pull the piece of glass out of my foot, and it hurt like hell!

I hobbled over to my Aunt Betty and Uncle Ernest's apartment and rang their doorbell. They fixed my foot, and fed me breakfast. Knowing the kid I was, I must have been pretty shaken up, because I was way too shy to just drop in somewhere. They were such kind friends and I missed our fun times up north. They were the friends who took Gigi when my mom went into the hospital. I missed my dog so much. I was happy that Gigi got to live in a safe home. In my thirties my psychologist made me realize that when my mom went into the hospital, not only was I was separated from my mom, but also my dog, sister, and dad. I never really thought about it since I was with Mimi and she was my safe place.

Since I was left alone so often, I liked living in an apartment. Being alone felt safer than having Priscilla or my dad around. My sane moments were listening to music, singing, dancing, and pretending I was famous. I loved Captain and Tennille "Love Will Keep Us Together", and "Tie A Yellow Ribbon", by Tony Orlando. Man I was cool! Music was my escape, leaving the world of fear for a world of fun and happiness. I would smile, laugh, and feel happy. I hear those songs now and I still smile.

Another great escape for me was the world of television. I will always remember the line up of shows, *Bewitched* being one of my favorites. I adored Tabatha and couldn't wait for an episode with her in it. Of course I wanted to be a witch, so I could make myself disappear or reappear. My other favorites were, *I Dream of Jennie*, *Gilligan's Island*, *The Brady Bunch*, and *The Partridge Family*.

In the middle of the school year, we moved into a house where the "fun" really began. I dreaded the end of a school day, even more than before. The house was big and scary and it always got dark before my dad eventually called. The end of the school day meant leaving my friends and going home alone. I would try to hint to friends, hoping they would invite me over and sometimes they did. Very often it was Leigh's home I would find myself at by the end of the evening. It became a routine of going home to an empty house, waiting and waiting, wondering what was going to happen. Sometimes Priscilla was home staggering around, other times she was passed out in bed. Other times she was nowhere to be found. It was always a mystery. Most evenings my dad would call me at home, looking for Priscilla. My dad would then call Leigh's mom, come home to pick me up and drop me off at their house, some nights to sleep, other nights for the evening. Many times he would take me driving while he looked for her. Once he found her, I would always pretend that I was asleep in the back seat, so they wouldn't ask me questions. My dad usually gave her crap, she usually yelled back, and the fighting would continue all the way home. Of course Priscilla was always drunk, and could never explain her whereabouts.

One day my dad told me Priscilla had a funeral to go to and, being Irish, she would be drinking a lot. I literally burst out laughing and asked how that would be different from any other day. Like seriously, are you kidding me? My dad had to go out, so a family friend Dawn came to babysit my friend Lara and me. Lara's dad and my dad were friends and what was really neat was that her cousin was a famous singer. We always got to sit in the front row at his concerts, and we also got to go backstage. I was too shy to say much, but it was very cool!

Poor Lara was exposed to Priscilla and her drunken nonsense a few times, but this night was the worst! It was almost six in the evening when Priscilla stumbled in yelling something. I realized she was calling me, but I didn't know what she wanted. Lara and I were terrified. We had no choice but to go upstairs to see what was going on. One look at her and I felt pure terror, she had blood all over her face and was yelling, asking why we were still awake. So we did what any normal ten-year-old kid would do, and ran upstairs as fast as we could shut the door, put a chair in front of it, jumping under the covers. We heard a knock on the door and we practically stopped breathing. It was Dawn, to make sure we were okay. She said not to be scared, that Priscilla wouldn't hurt us, she was just drunk and had walked into a tree. The next day my dad called me outside to look at Priscilla's face and head. He was asking ME why there wasn't a mark anywhere on her head or face!! Good job Dad, another great parenting choice.

We spent many weekends at our country home. The same home at which I spent weeks alone with my mom, but now I was with this crazy lady. This was my first exposure to Playgirl and Playboy magazines, which were always left around the house. I used to run around the woods by myself, stealing my dad's cigarettes and smoking little puffs, trying to be bad. They never noticed how long I was gone for, or the fact that I had cigarette breath, but at least I was away from their fighting and Priscilla's drunken banter.

The school year continued and there were more nights of screaming, yelling, fighting, and disappearing acts by Priscilla. One night the yelling was so bad I just started screaming: "I WANT TO GO LIVE WITH MIMI, I WANT TO GO LIVE WITH MIMI"! My father came in and told me to stop screaming. Really? I was sobbing and all he could do was go back to his room yelling at Priscilla, telling her that she was making his daughter want to go live elsewhere. Once again, great job Dad.

On the last morning of grade four, I woke up at Leigh's. On the way to school, Leigh and I walked to my house to pick up some games to play. As we were approaching my house there were cars everywhere. I told Leigh that it looked like a funeral. I walked in the front door to find my house full of people. When my dad saw me walk in, he told me that Priscilla had committed suicide in our garage. I had to go outside to tell Leigh that I wouldn't be going to school with her. Poor kid, looking back she was probably really upset. I feel bad that I left her to walk to school by herself.

Finding out Priscilla was dead didn't make me feel sad, I was relieved. Then I felt guilty that I wasn't sad, which was very confusing for me. I went up to my room and held the teddy bear my mom had left me, I don't ever remember holding it before that time. I finally felt like things would be better and knowing Mimi was coming to pick me up, made me happy. I was also grateful for not being the one who found her body. I was freaked out enough just knowing that she killed herself in our garage.

I spent the weekend with Mimi and Helen, which was great. My sister would be coming home from boarding school, and that made me very happy too. We had to go to the "wake" at our house. All I remember from that event was my dad introducing me to Marsha, Harvey and their two-year-old daughter Christie. She followed me around everywhere and we quickly became friends. Good thing because my dad informed me that they were going to move in with us. Weird, but whatever! To me they were strangers and now they were going to be living with us. At least they seemed like nice people, and Christie was like a little playmate for me.

A New Family: 1975

LIVING WITH MARSHA, HARVEY, AND Christie was a blessing because they were such good people. Marsha took good care of us, I had fun with Christie, and one of the best parts was that my sister was back home. Monica and I shared a bedroom, and I finally felt like I had a family. We still lived at the house in which Priscilla committed suicide, but nobody seemed to care. Christie and I played, and I loved fixing her hair. I was not always patient, so I remember pulling at her hair if she would move; looking back I feel so bad for doing that. Christie just loved having me do things for her, so she didn't seem to care.

I had a few friends that were boys. This was the beginning of not understanding how boys think. These boys who were supposed to be my friends, one day they would be throwing snowballs at me, or on another day they would ring my doorbell to play tag. One boy even choked me with a chain until some lady came running over whacking him with her purse. Marsha told me that boys acted like this, when they liked a girl. That was very confusing to me.

My grade five teacher had a positive impact on my life. She used to call me "Shana bubbila". Looking back she probably felt sorry for me, but she will never know just how much she positively affected my life. I've tried to find her recently but had no luck; I would have loved for her to know the positive impact she had on me. I was unable to concentrate very well in school, shocking, I know. In grade four I got a report card with my first bad marks. I got "has difficulty" in both geography and history. I was so upset, hearing all my friends talk about how their parents would kill them if they brought home a bad report card. I was scared, and I figured my dad would be mad, but he never saw it. I told him I got it, but he never asked to see it, so I never showed it to him. I signed it myself and brought it back to school. I was very unhappy with my "HD" in geography and history, and hated both subjects ever since. The one thing I was really good at was spelling. For some reason I could see the words, hear them, and visualize how to spell all of them correctly. My teacher gave me the job of taking students outside the classroom to help them. I felt so proud, and it was a very positive experience, thanks to my teacher.

The crazy thing is how long this negativity about geography and history has stuck with me. For years and years, the mention of those subjects would give me anxiety, and make me feel like I was stupid. As I got older I realized that how we learn and what we know does not define our intelligence. We all have the ability to learn, and the ability to gain knowledge. What we do with the knowledge is what matters.

Of course my dad had to disrupt the calm life my sister and I were living. He forced me to go to our country house with his new girlfriend, and her two sons. I had a bad feeling, possibly just fear from the past experiences. All I know is that I did not want another new family, but something told me I would have no choice. Grade five ended and sadly so did our time with Marsha, Harvey and Christie. I don't even remember saying goodbye or moving. Life was about to change once again.

Stepmother #2-Broom Hilda: 1976-1979

ONCE AGAIN I HAD TO start a new school. This stepmother was a whole different kind of "cray cray" from Priscilla. She was the typical, mean stepmother depicted in some movies, her kids came first and my sister and I were treated very poorly. My sister hated her. The feeling was most probably mutual, so Monica would stay away, spending a lot of time with her boyfriend's family. I missed her.

We moved into a new house in an expensive area, probably because this new wife was all about living the high life. I began grade six at another new school. Once again I had to make new friends, which always made me nervous. On top of it, "Broom Hilda" had a mission to lower my self-esteem to a level that would take me years to recover from, if ever. For some reason I would still vye for her attention. There was a part of me that just wanted to have a mom, and feel somewhat normal. That was not at all what she had in mind.

How many ways are there to lower a girls self esteem? I think this stepmother had a book on it. I was entering puberty, and Broom Hilda did not make this a pleasant experience. One day right in front of my dad, she started laughing and pointing at my chest, saying she could see my nipples. Was I mortified? One could say that, but wait, it gets worse. Once she came up for air, she said that I had to start wearing a bra. She trotted off to her room, and then handed me one of her old bras that didn't fit her anymore. She threw it at me saying, "Here, try this". Off I went, being the obedient kid I was, and I put it on. When I came back down, she was hysterical all over again. She found it very funny that she could see my bra. She also said "at least now that your boobs are growing, they will balance out your big butt". This totally crushed me. For the next twenty-two years, I only wore baggy shirts, or sweatshirts, and made darn sure nobody could see my bra or my boobs. My insecurities were born, my self-esteem crushed, and although I only weighed 105 lbs., I now felt fat.

My next big event arrived, and Broom Hilda was not going to make this pleasant either. Thank goodness my sister was there. We were up at our country home, and I was in so much pain that I thought I was dying. But, it was just that time of the month. Broom Hilda was her usual self. My father and his friends were sitting around the dining room table. Broom Hilda threw a box of sanitary pads at me and said, "here you go Elizabeth, have a period party". *YES!* I thought, just what I wanted to do, I really wanted to share this with my dad and his friends! Needless to say, that stunted the oncoming of another period for two years. I guess I could thank her for that…

Grade seven was awful. I had to go to a French school, and I never quite mastered the language. Throw in the fact that I was shy, and had a strange retainer that was two inches thick on the top and bottom of my mouth. It was gross, and made me talk with a giant lisp. I had to use a key to screw it open every week. On top of it I needed glasses, talk about feeling like the biggest geek!

Grade eight began in a new home and new school. I found my new high school frightening. There were so many more kids than I was used to. I didn't know anyone, the kids seemed tougher, and it was very intimidating for me. Slowly I met some friends, but Rachel and I became the closest. Her parents were divorced and that was difficult for her. We shared stories, and I told her how Broom Hilda always treated her own sons so much better than she treated me. Even at that young age, I knew that this stepmother liked the financial benefits of being with my dad.

Rachel suggested we try out for the badminton team, which I thought would be fun. I tried so hard, and I played the best I could, to the point where my arm was hurting. I got home after practice and Hilda laughed at the mention of me being on a Badminton team. I felt awful, the muscles in my arm were hurting from playing for two hours, and now I felt as though it had been for nothing. The next day at school, Rachel and I found out that we made the team. We were so excited, and my first thought was now I could tell Hilda that I *did* make the team. Once in gym class, the teacher apologized and told me that because of my birth date, I couldn't be on the team. I had to try out with the older kids, which I did not want to do. I was crushed, but I held back my tears. Hilda was no comfort at all, in fact, she didn't even believe me when I told her that I had made the team.

My gym teacher that year was a lady I will never forget. We were doing some of the endurance testing, and we had to run around the track. I ran with ease. I didn't think much of it, but she did. She actually pulled me aside to tell me that I had great endurance, and she wanted me to try out for the cross-country running team. I felt so proud. Her words and compliment stayed with me. I went home and was excited to share the news. Why I bothered, I will never know. Hilda laughed once again; how could I go try out now? So I never did.

Many years later in 2013, at the Las Vegas airport, I bumped into that same gym teacher. I knew there was no way she would know me, but I recognized her right away. I went right up to her to introduce myself. She had just retired, and I told her how that one compliment stuck with me and how much of a difference it made. She thanked me for sharing that, saying it really meant a great deal to her. The feeling was mutual.

The years with Hilda were special, and I don't mean that in a positive way. The worst thing of all was that she would not allow me to see Mimi, and I was always forced to spend the weekends up north. Some of the weekends were actually fun. My stepbrothers were not all that bad, and we did play games together. The weekends I was allowed to go see Mimi were always the best. Mimi loved to feed me my favorite Lebanese meals, but if I ever brought food home, Broom Hilda would throw it out! When I wanted to make Mimi's delicious salad, she had a fit and threw me out of the kitchen. She bought her sons whatever clothes they wanted, but not me. I had this huge closet, with two pairs of pants and two sweaters. I was not allowed to buy jeans or the Adidas running shoes that I wanted so badly. Granted, at least I had clothes, but seriously? My friend Rachel suggested I speak to a guidance counselor at the school, who had helped her a lot. It did feel good speaking with an adult. This was my first experience with therapy, and it is amazing that I ever trusted another therapist again.

A few weeks later at dinner, Hilda was flying high on her broom. She wouldn't look at me, or talk to me. I had no idea what I had done. I was feeling sick, with a sore throat, but she didn't care. She made it clear that the cleaning lady was coming the next day, and everyone had to go to school, no matter what. Clearly, that was directed at me. The next morning I felt worse. I was pretty sick, with fever and was awaken by my father and Hilda fighting. And there it was. Hilda was screaming at my dad and was mad because she found out I had spoken to the guidance counselor at school. I was not pleased and was confused as to how she found out. The counselor told my stepbrother, who of course told his mother. I couldn't believe my ears. Hilda was fuming! My father came into my room and of course was not on my side. All he could do was ask why I would go talk to a stranger about our life, and then asked if I needed money. I was sick in bed, my stepmother hated me, and somehow he thought money was going to help?!

So it began. Two weeks of insults under her breath as she walked by me, or she would pretend I was invisible, sometimes walking into me on purpose giving me a little shove, not saying a word. Wow, how mature! This was not the outcome I expected after putting my trust in a counselor. Needless to say I never went back. How could this counselor talk to my stepbrother? I was nervous, and I hated going home even more, and just wanted to be back at Mimi's.

Mid-week, one day before dinner, I went home and just wanted to have a shower. All of a sudden "Broomy" was banging on the bathroom door, yelling at me to get out. *Um. No!* She continued and continued, so I caved. I wrapped a towel around myself and came out. She looked enraged! I guess she expected me to react during the two weeks of bad treatment, but I had not. So she was done, she was yelling and screaming at me, saying that I was a horrible person for talking to a stranger and blah blah blah... I had never seen her so angry. I finally reacted when she raised her hand to smack me across the face. I grabbed her arm, which seemed to surprise her. I had reached my limit with all of her abuse. I told her that if she dared touch me, she would be sorry. I'm not sure what I would've done, but I guess we could have scrapped it out. Nothing stopped her bantering. It was when she said the words; "you killed your mother and now you are going to kill your father"! That was when I lashed back and screamed, "How did I kill my mother? And if anyone kills my father it will be you". I was so angry and by this time, I walked out of the bathroom knowing she would follow me. As she came after me I turned, brushed my shoulder against hers, throwing her off balance. This gave me the opportunity to run back into the bathroom and lock the door. I got back in the shower, letting the warm water soothe me as I stood there shaking like a leaf. Thinking of her words about my mother, I began to cry, and then I was sobbing wondering, *how did I kill my mother?*

Once I got out and dressed, I heard my dad calling me from downstairs. Shockingly enough he wasn't on my side and asked me; why did you yell at Hilda? Why were you rude? You should apologize. You shouldn't have shared private things from our home with a stranger. Hilda's a good person. Why can't we just have peace and harmony? I finally stood up to him and spoke "Really Dad? Peace and harmony"? Through my tears I continued, "she was the one who tried to hit me, she was yelling at me, telling me I am the reason my mom is dead and somehow I am going to kill you too!" Hilda stood there and lied, saying she never said any of those things. I was furious, but in the end I felt as though I had won. She stormed out, and my dad finally agreed that I could go visit Mimi for the weekend. Yippee!

Weekends at Mimi's were always the best. This particular weekend was the most amazing. Saturday evening, Mimi, Helen, and I were watching television when the doorbell rang. I couldn't believe it, it was my father. He came up the stairs looking very upset. I had a selfish sick thought that maybe Broom Hilda had killed herself too. Then I heard my dad say, "I left Hilda", and with those words, I immediately shrieked with happiness. Helen and I went into the kitchen to leave Mimi and my dad talk.

I was so happy because on top of everything, I got to stay at Mimi's. School was about to end and I knew that the summer would be so much better. My sister and I were "permitted" one hour in "our" own home, to go get our belongings. Helen drove us, and we sat like spies waiting for Broom Hilda to leave the house. We were all nervous and giddy. Once she drove away, we got out of the car and went into the house. Hilda's son was there to be sure we didn't "steal" anything. We were shocked to find that my diamond earrings, a gift from Mimi, were gone, which I knew had been in my drawer. Of course my dad didn't believe me, he said that I must've lost them, but I knew better.

I love the process of life and the wisdom, which comes along with growing older. In my thirties I realized at last, that this stepmother was the one who was so insecure. She hated my youth, and was probably insecure about her age and body. Nonetheless, the insecurities about my own body have plagued me for years. There was too much damage done through her words. I always wore baggy clothes to cover my breasts, and felt fat even when I was a perfect weight for my height and age, thanks to Broomy.

Life With Our Aunt & Uncle: 1979

ANOTHER NEW BEGINNING WITH THE start of grade nine. My sister, my dad, and I went to live with my aunt and uncle. When I was much younger, I know we spent time with them and my first cousins. I have little snapshots of memories but after my mom died I don't remember seeing them much at all. Then again memories are few and far between.

As excited, as I was that I was no longer dealing with my stepmother, I was also quite nervous. I was shy and even though I was going to see some old friends, I also knew I was coming into a new school once again. Everyone else had built friendships throughout the years while I wasn't there.

Leigh met me on the first day with some other friends. I felt better knowing a few kids. One of the first "new" friends I met was Tasha. She was loud and gave me a bit of a headache, but she laughed a lot. She told me very clearly that Tasha was pronounced *Taw-sha not Ta-sha*. Tasha's birthday party was coming up that weekend. I heard the girls talking about it, but I wasn't invited. Being ultra sensitive, I immediately felt like crying, and felt left out. The other girls were really sweet and they said they would talk to Tasha. Long story short, she wasn't allowed to have one more person, but in the end, she did extend the invitation.

So the school year began. Friendships were made. Nine of us formed a little group of friends, and we all had a lot of fun together. Looking back I realize how fortunate I was to have met them as well as so many other wonderful people. High school can be a very difficult time for many, and although there was normal drama, these girls became my good friends. They accepted me with all my moods, even though they didn't always understand how subtle things that were said could send my mood spiraling downward. One of them could have mentioned shopping with their mom, and my mood would instantly change. I was so moody, and I never liked that about myself. I knew that somehow, I had to change. Even though I had Mimi and her love, it was never the same as having my own mom to do mother/daughter things with. Later in years, I realized, having a real mother is not always better. I have heard stories about how much damage some parents do to their kids. I count my blessing every day.

Tasha and I became really good friends with Jade, who was a year older. My first experience with alcohol was with the two of them. We shared a bottle of Baby Duck, because it was the only alcohol we could buy from the corner store. We were obviously desperate since we broke the bottle on the sidewalk because we didn't have a bottle opener. We were determined to go to our school dance tipsy, so we did. We always had lots of laughs together.

We only lived with my aunt and uncle while my dad was trying to find us another home. We were thrilled when my dad told us that he rented a home for Mimi, Helen, and all of us to live in together. I didn't really care if my dad was there, and to be honest the memories I have from this time in my life, don't really include him.

Home at Last: 1980–1982

I N GRADE TEN I WAS introduced to Luke at a party. Our dads were really good friends, but we'd never met, until now. He went to a different school and was a year older. We just clicked: first love is always special. He lived further away, so he would take a taxi to come over on weekends. We would do silly things like bake together. Mimi and Helen nicknamed us Betty and Duncan, like Betty Crocker and Duncan Hines.

We also shared so much, and he would cry to me many times over some of the problems he was having. His mom had also passed away and his life was difficult. He was such a nice guy, but life was not easy. It felt good to be such close friends and be able to share so much. I really, really liked Luke, the butterfly-kind-of-like at that age. We spoke on the phone a lot. My friend Tasha kept saying we would get married one day. I never slept with him, or never did much because I was always scared. I didn't know why at that point in time, and he was never pushy.

A few months passed, Luke and I were happy, so I thought. My dad had a condo on the beach in Florida, and he always let me invite a friend. During Christmas break we enjoyed the beach, pool days, and shopping. I remember being very excited to get home to see Luke. He came to visit me right away, but something was different, he was different. I didn't know what it was, but I knew something was wrong. He kept apologizing saying that he didn't want to hurt me. My heart was breaking. What had he done? He told me that he loved me, and then he finally said it - he slept with someone while I was in Florida. Followed by the words, it didn't mean anything.... blah blah blah. My heart broke, I cried for hours, for days, for weeks. He kept calling me apologizing. I wanted to forgive him and I wanted to forget, but I couldn't.

I finally caved, and took him back. But now he didn't have the old me. I was no fun, and I couldn't give him my heart. I was still hurt, I couldn't forget. I definitely was not going to sleep with him. I felt as though the reason he cheated on me was because I hadn't slept with him yet. I still couldn't go there, and I finally broke up with him. He was mad and felt that I only got back together with him to hurt him. He didn't get it, he broke my heart and broke something else inside of me as well. I would never be the same with him. I would never forget. For now, this was the end of Luke. I began to realize that after Luke broke my heart, a pattern began. I started dating other guys throughout the next two years. I never slept with any of them, and as soon as the relationship started getting too serious, I ended it.

A year later Luke called me, right before his grade eleven grad. He wanted me to be his date. With the pain gone, I was kind of excited. The only problem was that I was in bed with tonsillitis. At that time in my life I got sick almost every month. Luke kept in touch with my sister daily, and in the end after much begging on my part, I was allowed to go. My sister took me shopping for an outfit, and off we went to Luke's grad. We had fun, but somehow by morning we ended up in a fight, and that was that. Looking back I am sure he was expecting that typical "grad night", but it didn't happen, so maybe he was frustrated. I will never know for sure.

My dad was barely around, which was fine. Mimi always welcomed my friends, we had sleepovers which were always so much fun. Mimi always kept a cupboard devoted to junk food for me, and my friends.

Everyone knew where to go, and Helen would buy us more treats, not that we needed them. We had eaten everything from chips, cheezies, pretzels, corn puffs, candy, chocolate, popsicles, ice cream, and even pizza. By the end of the evening we all felt sick thinking about it. We would all be moaning while complaining how full we were. It didn't stop us from waking up in the morning, and grabbing a slice of cold pizza out of the box.

Summer after grade ten Tasha and I worked at a sleep away camp. We were too young to be counselors so we were hired as kitchen staff. We hated it, and were going to quit. We were being asked why we were working as kitchen scum, and that it didn't suit us. Isn't that mean? In any case we ended up becoming friends with the counselors, and had a blast.

The summer began so rocky at the camp, and also on a personal level for me. One of the first nights, Tasha and I were trying to sleep when a few of the girls came in totally drunk. I was scared to death, not understanding why this was so terrifying to me. Then I realized that the fear was from memories of the past. I lay awake for some time. Everyone else was sleeping when I heard our cabin door open. Then I heard footsteps, and I was terrified. One of the older male staff members was walking very quietly towards my bed. When he sat down on my bed, I froze. My heart was beating out of my chest. I could not speak or move. What the hell did he want? Then I felt his hand on my breast. He was breathing heavy and now so was I, but for a totally different reason. I couldn't move. He took my hand, and put it on his crotch. I felt sick. I tried to pull my hand away, but he held it firmly in place. I was praying Tasha would wake up. He either realized I wasn't enjoying this experience, or realized how disgusting he was, but thankfully he got up and left. I buried my head into my pillow and cried until I finally fell asleep.

The next day I told Tasha. Somehow we even had the nerve to go right up to him and I looked at him and said, "what the heck were you thinking? Are you crazy?" I was terrified. What a guy! He looked at me claiming to have no idea what I was talking about. I was furious and confused. It was greatly satisfying years later when I saw him again, and he actually apologized. He was trying to say he was wrong to take advantage of me knowing I was vulnerable, and how sorry he was. I was happy to tell him to "fuck off" in no uncertain terms, and that he was a total asshole. That felt great!

Grade eleven was as good as it gets. From my group of friends, some of us spent less time with school work, and more time on all the committees. We planned winter carnival, our grad, took part in the variety show, and still had fun doing our other things like skiing, and partying. On June 6th, 1982, as the school year was coming to end, I was baking Mimi her birthday cake when my dad decided to come home, to give Monica and I some news. He told us that he was moving in with his new girlfriend and wanted my sister and I to move in with them. He was a comedian, because there was no way we were moving in with him, and his fourth wife! My sister and I were not going to budge on that. I was so angry and to make matters worse, he distracted me so much, that I burned Mimi's cake. Once again he was ruining everything! It didn't matter that we were happy, he was making plans to move once again, regardless of what we might want.

College: 1983–1985

E VEN THOUGH MY DAD MADE the decision that it was time to move again, there was a bright side. Monica and I were going to live with Mimi and Helen in their old neighborhood. There was a bedroom in the basement that would be mine, with my own bathroom, which was pretty cool. Mimi, Helen and my sister each had their own bedroom upstairs. My dad was moving in with his girlfriend.

I was dreading college because it meant more change. All my close friends were going to different schools. Luckily in grade eleven I became friends with Ronni. Even though throughout high school we knew each other, we had different groups of friends. It was Ronni who asked me if I wanted to go to the college open house together. I was nervous to go on my own, so I was thrilled. Ronni and I became the best of friends, and our friendship remains strong to this day. Ronni has always been one of my dearest, most trusted friends. We are the same age, with our birthdays only five days apart. We have been through many things together, always able to share anything, knowing that we will always be there for each other no matter what.

My sister was getting a new car, so I was given her Camaro. Having a car at that age without the financial worry was amazing. Even though I had financial security, it didn't mean I was truly happy. Many people perceived me as the spoiled princess who had everything, although

Ronni knew differently. I was able to pick Ronni up for school on many days. She put up with my smoking in the car, my anger issues, and all the nonsense that came along with me at that age. I was a mess and didn't even know it. Ronni stuck by me through it all.

My dad announced that he was getting married during the summer. They were hosting the wedding at his new country home. I was going to be at sleep away camp with Ronni and thought it was the perfect excuse to miss this big event. My dad insisted and I felt I had no choice. The photographer got a picture of me making a face during the ceremony. Who could blame me? Ronni was with me and we enjoyed the free flowing Champagne. So much so, that we jumped in the pool with our clothes on. I am pretty sure the adults were not impressed. Once we got out of the pool, Ronni walked up to my new stepmom and sat on her lap. I could not contain my hysterical laughter, because my stepmom shrieked and was not impressed saying how expensive her dress was. I was quite pleased. My night ended passed out in one of the bedrooms until it was time to go home.

During my first year in college I woke up one night with a high fever, and in a lot of pain. My fever would not break, and the next day, Mimi and my sister took me to the doctor. My appendix could have ruptured, so I was brought to the hospital for emergency surgery. I was scared, but Mimi and my sister were there, and even my dad showed up. He offered to buy the doctors food as I was being wheeled into the elevator for surgery, which made me laugh. That was my dad, always offering food to people.

I will never forget waking up after the surgery, what a strange feeling. I couldn't cough or move without searing pain in my abdomen. My health issues were just beginning, although I had no idea at the time. This easy surgery to remove my appendix ended up being a much longer process. I was supposed to be released two days after the surgery, but instead, because I developed an infection, I had to stay in the hospital for ten days.

At this point in my life I hated school, and had even entertained the idea of dropping out. Now I had no choice but to drop the entire semester, because I had missed too many classes. I was off school for almost three months, totally bored out of my mind. Going back to school was something I could not wait to do. This experience was my first of many lessons of how, "Everything Happens For a Reason." Not that I wanted appendicitis, but the time off really made me see how much I wanted and needed to be in school.

Months passed and Luke came back into my life very briefly. He took me on a fun date to an amusement park nearby. He did all those romantic things, won me prizes at the games, made me laugh, and we had a great time. Then I didn't hear from him for about a year, which I couldn't understand. I still had a great deal to learn about men.

During this year, a family friend did the unthinkable. To me this guy was like a big brother, especially because he used to call me his little sister. I loved him like a brother, until the night he came into my room. I was shocked, and once again I froze. I hated myself for that. I could not move as he put his hands all over me. I don't remember him doing much, but when he finally left, I began to shake and cry. I didn't understand and I hated myself for not yelling, kicking, or punching him. I felt absolutely horrible. Aside from feeling violated, I could not understand why I didn't move, why I became paralyzed, and couldn't speak. Of course years later, and through therapy session after therapy session, I came to understand the pattern. Of course I froze, and didn't move. It was ingrained in me; it was what I had been taught to do, at a very young age.

The next day I was in a horrible mood. When I saw him I felt sick, especially because he acted as of nothing happened. He even went as far as to ask why I was so grumpy. I was so angry. I could not understand why all these men were behaving this way. I confided in one person who told me that I must have asked for it in some way. Who ever asks to be violated? So I never told anyone until many years later. The reaction was still the same. I always felt judged, and very misunderstood, which felt terrible.

I did not understand my sexuality, nor was I having sex with anyone. I always froze when anything got physical. I didn't understand why I was so terrified of having sex, but it wasn't something that I was opposed to trying. I had boyfriends, but sexually, things never went too far. During this time an older man was flirting with me, and although I thought it was innocent, there was nothing innocent about it on his part. My vulnerability, and my "daddy issues" must have been obvious. At first it was more of an emotional affair, then it became more. I only realized later in years that he actually waited until I was over eighteen to make a move. This is something that I'm not proud of, and have been living with guilt and pain for years. I hated myself for doing it, knowing it was wrong. I would end it, and then I would go back. Over the years I shared this with many friends. My true friends never judged me, and always stood by me, while others did not. These are the defining moments in life, when you find out who your true friends really are.

The worst part was that it robbed me from having normal relationships throughout those years. All of my conscious experiences left me with a huge mistrust in men. After all, my first boyfriend cheated on me, this man was cheating on his wife, and I had been violated many times. It's surprising that I've ever been able to have a normal relationship, and that I ever trusted anyone enough to get married. My desperate need for a family, and the huge void inside of me, was bigger than anything else.

My father had been living in a condo with his new wife. They were buying a house together, so my dad offered the condo to my sister, and me. I was sad to be leaving Mimi and Helen, but then again it seemed to make sense for us to be on our own. At this point I was seventeen, and my sister was twenty-three. For the most part it was great, and I had the freedom to do what I wanted. Our dad provided for us financially, he bought me a new car, even though I never asked for one. Once again many people just saw me as a spoiled kid, although having riches didn't make me feel rich. I had a void in me that even I didn't understand, often feeling very alone. Looking back I realize that other people had a perception of me, basing the quality of my life on all of these materialistic things. I definitely did not have a bad life. I did feel very fortunate, but the materialistic things didn't fill my need to be loved, and to have a family.

My past was in the past, but I still didn't understand a lot about myself. The things that were happening to me affected me deeply, and it began to come out on a physical level. I had been taken to the hospital twice for unexplained fevers, and severe abdominal pain. I was put on antibiotics, but never had a clear answer as to what the infections were. During one of my stays, I was woken during the night by an orderly who tried to put his hand up my hospital gown. I was terrified and felt that paralyzing fear once again. Obviously, he thought I was sedated, and didn't think I would wake up. I jolted once I felt his hand coming up my leg, which must have scared him because he left suddenly. I rang for the nurse, but she felt that I must have been dreaming. Again, I felt so frustrated, alone, scared, and misunderstood. I was lying in a hospital bed, knowing I wasn't asking to be violated, so why did this keep happening?

Luke came back into my life very briefly, calling me to ask me out on a date. During this date, he confessed that he regretted that we never had sex. Now I knew why he wanted this date. I always cared about Luke, but I was cautious. I was nineteen by now and wasn't planning on going to dinner, and then straight to his bed. I guess he was hoping it would go that way. I also had a feeling that either way, I wouldn't see him again for a long time. My instincts were correct.

College was ending and I had no idea what to apply for in University. I had filled out forms to go into Psychology, but that just didn't feel right. I called Ronni since she was already at University in Physical Education, and loving it. She told me I would love it too, and since I trusted her, I ripped up my application and applied to Physical Education. She was right, I did love it.

A few more years passed, and Luke reappeared. We ran into each other and he told me that he was getting married. I was happy for him, but there was a strange feeling that I couldn't explain. I still cared a lot about him, and I felt my heart sink when he said he was getting married; especially because it was the girl he cheated on me with. But I was happy for him more than anything.

About six months later I heard that Luke was in the hospital. He had been in a horrific accident, after only being married for a short time. He had gone out and then realized he forgot something at home. He arrived home realizing that he didn't have his keys, so he climbed onto the roof where he grabbed a ladder to get into his apartment. The ladder hit a live wire, which tragically electrocuted Luke. He was badly burned and was in the hospital barely clinging to his life. We all gathered at a Church service to pray for him. He was a great guy, his life just beginning. How does this happen? A few days later my sister came into my room to wake me with the news. Luke had died at such a young age, what a loss. We cried in each other's arms. I hated death.

Endings & Beginnings: 1986–1994

I N MY TWENTIES, LIKE MANY people I thought I knew everything. Looking back, I know how wrong I was. I was in my second year of University, which is when I met my husband Neil. It was an exciting time. I knew I wanted a family so very badly and I couldn't wait to have my own kids.

By now the affair I had been having, was over. I had always been open about it and never tried to hide it. I felt the need to tell Neil, he didn't react, saying that he could see how these things could happen. I didn't really know who I was yet, nor did I remember exactly what I had been through. I felt better being open about my past, and yet something inside me told me it was a mistake.

Our relationship began, and we did everything a normal couple would do. We went on our first trip together on Christmas day in 1987. My dad had tried calling to wish me Merry Christmas, but I missed his call. I tried to call him back but there was no answer, so off we went to the airport. We went to Jamaica for two weeks to an all-inclusive resort.

We had a fun trip except for one day in particular, when I couldn't shake a bad feeling that I had. The night before I had a dream about Luke's funeral, and my dad. The next day I didn't feel right, but I assumed it was just from having the bad dream, which brought back the memories of a sad time.

I remember coming home very clearly. It was an over night flight. Neil asked for our city newspaper, but they didn't have any left. We arrived home at 7:30 a.m. the next morning. My sister and cousin picked us up from the airport. They were both acting weird. We got in the car, and they kept chatting, asking all kinds of questions. I asked how everyone was doing, and they both answered awkwardly at the same time. They were bringing us to visit Mimi. I was now officially worried, "Is Mimi ok? It's so early I can go see her later." They would not hear of it, we had to go right away, so I knew something was wrong.

Helen was awake, and their cleaning lady who was there also seemed to be acting strange. Helen guided Neil into the kitchen, while my sister brought me into Mimi's room. I was just happy Mimi was there, and alive. I was terrified something had happened to her. When I hugged her she started to cry. She kept saying how much she missed me. I missed her too, but I was home now. Things were racing through my mind. I was sure they were going to tell me that Mimi was sick. Why else would she be crying like this? Then finally they came out with it. My dad had a heart attack while he was in Miami. So I asked, "where is he, can we go see him"? My sister started to cry, telling me that he didn't survive, and that he died in Miami. Of course I began to cry, except it was very strange. I cried for a few minutes and then stopped. I remember my sister telling me that it was okay to cry, but something in me shut down. I refused to be sad. Luckily I hadn't seen the newspaper on the airplane, because when Neil opened it at Mimi's, my dad's picture and obituary were in that edition.

The family had waited to have the funeral. I remember feeling like I should be sad, although there were times I did cry, I still couldn't even explain my emotions. One of the strangest moments was when we got to the cemetery, and we were standing at the grave sight. My stepmother was mortified that my dad was being buried in the same plot as my mom, sharing the same tombstone. I felt strange seeing my mother's tombstone for the first time. Seeing her name was a little shocking even for me, and realizing that I had never even seen it before made me cry.

After the funeral, my sister, and I went to Mimi's. I don't even remember what the rest of the family did, but it didn't involve my sister, or me. We were sitting around Mimi's kitchen table, and I was feeling strange not sure what we were supposed to be doing. I decided that I would go back to school the next day, which surprised my sister. I didn't see any point in sitting at home. I preferred getting back to life. Going back to school, being with friends, that just seemed like the right thing to do.

Neil was supportive, especially considering he had never experienced losing anyone. I was also acting very strange about the whole situation. I went on about life as if nothing had happened. My sister was having a more difficult time, since she was a lot closer to our dad. I was dealing with such conflict, but didn't understand it. Unfortunately at that time my sister and I were fighting a lot, and there were issues with my dad's will and testament. It was not a fun time.

My dad and uncle had built their business, but over the years my dad wasn't as active in the business. He was too busy leaving all winter, living in Florida with his new wife. Dealing with my dad's will and estate became somewhat of an eighteen-month nightmare. Our dad left us shares in his business, and although it was all in black and white, somehow it didn't seem quite fair. We felt our only option was to hire lawyers, even though we weren't sure we could change any of it, we decided to try anyway. The only family we had left, our aunt, uncle, and cousins, felt that we attacked them in fighting for what we felt was more fair regarding a business our father started. This changed our relationship with them forever.

By now I was twenty-two, and Neil's lease was coming to an end, so we moved in together. My sister and I were fighting quite a bit and I felt it was a good time to move out so each of us could have our own space. About a year later, Neil and I got engaged. I was more eager for us to get married, since I couldn't wait to have kids and a family of my own. This desire was bigger than me.

Given that Mimi had been my lifeline, I asked her to give me away at my wedding. I rarely saw my aunt and uncle or any of the family, but somehow, not asking my uncle became a cardinal sin. I felt terrible. He was very hurt, and I really didn't understand it. I went to see my aunt and uncle to try to explain, but I was told I was being very disrespectful. I cried and cried. I just couldn't do it. Mimi had been elated when I asked her, we even cried together. Our bond was so strong, and she had been there for me every single time life got terrible. Thinking back I can't help but wonder why they didn't both walk me down the aisle. I honestly can't even remember if it was even suggested. Mimi was going to walk me down the aisle, and what should have been a very happy time, became a very unpleasant experience. On top of it, I was shocked that nobody thought about how I may have been feeling. I was in my mid twenties, getting married and both my parents were dead. I wasn't harping on it, but instead was thrilled that I had Mimi to walk me down the aisle. How could anyone make me feel bad for that?

It was a small wedding at a golf course. I wasn't the typical bride, and I really could not be bothered with all the planning. I asked Helen to pick the flowers, given she was a floral designer. Shirley was a jeweler, so I asked her to design the rings. For the meal, I almost had my sister's mother in law take care of it, but it was suggested I go to the golf course, to try some of their food myself. Reluctantly I did. My sister stepped in and offered to buy me my wedding dress and to help me have one made.

I don't remember everything, but I do remember making a short speech thanking Mimi for being there for me my whole life. When I was done, I noticed my entire family except for one cousin, were getting up to leave. I really didn't think much of it until I went in the hallway, and heard another cousin screaming at them outside. I went over to see them all getting in their cars without a good bye. Somehow I had done the unthinkable, from not asking my uncle to give me away, to not thanking them.... and the icing on the cake was that they assumed I placed them at a table behind a pillar, on purpose. Seriously? The very sad thing to me was that I actually put some thought into that table seating. I never saw the pillar in the seating chart and I actually took the time to seat my family close to the front. They left, and I cried in my cousin's arms. I thanked him and his wife for staying. He said we would need to talk when I got back from my honeymoon, but that never happened.

I fell asleep crying, woke up crying feeling sad and hurt. I was still crying as our flight took off on our way to Arizona for our honeymoon. This was not how I was expecting to start the life I was dreaming of living.

In my mid twenties I was married, and thought I was happy. I was quite oblivious to how much my childhood had affected me. Neil was a really good guy, but neither one of us knew how to communicate that well. He grew up in a family that really didn't talk about their feelings. I was very independent and would never ask for help even if I needed it. On an emotional level, I always acted as though I didn't need anybody.

Before we had kids, we did a lot of things separately. Neil golfed every weekend while I slept in and made plans with friends. January 1992 I found out that I was pregnant. I was ecstatic, and Neil was happy too, but more nervous than anything. My sister was also pregnant, which meant I would be an aunt first, and that was very exciting. During my pregnancy, I ate a lot and gained quite a bit of weight. I wasn't feeling great about myself. The day Neil looked at me and asked if I was going to lose the weight after I had the baby, was the day something in my heart changed. That comment crushed me to the core. He had no idea the impact that those words would have in our marriage, and even though he later tried to apologize, those words broke something inside of me.

I went through the summer, working with a friend at a summer day camp. We did all the hiring, and scheduling together in the winter, and during the summer, we were on our feet all day. During this time, Neil wasn't too supportive or patient with my discomfort. I was becoming very unhappy. Although I was excited to have this baby, I felt like a beached whale, and emotionally I felt alone.

Once I gave birth, I wasn't sure I could ever go through that again. I wasn't one of those women who thought the experience was so beautiful. It terrified me, especially because the baby was not coming out! After twenty-four hours of labor and hours of pushing, the doctor told me to stop. Suddenly an oxygen mask was placed on my face, and four nurses appeared. There were two of them on either side of me and all at once they all put their hands on my belly and jumped. They pushed so hard that my upper body flew up and I felt winded. Happily Samantha swooshed out! She didn't cry at first, and she was very blue. Finally the sound of her little cry was a huge relief, and made me cry tears of joy.

After giving birth, I didn't feel well at all. When I was finally wheeled out and saw Neil's parents, Monica, and Mimi, I felt relieved, but I had a fever and couldn't stop shaking. The nurse brought Samantha to us, and my sister and I looked at her little hands, which were still blue. That scared me, but Monica quickly wrapped them back up, and told me not to worry. Once everyone left, the nurse brought Samantha into the nursery and I went to sleep for a little while. A few hours later the nurse came to wake me to feed Samantha. Although I was excited to see my new baby, I was also nervous. The first feeding didn't go well, Samantha started choking, and then had projectile vomiting. I was actually scared that there was something wrong.

The next morning Neil came to pick us up to bring us home. I can't even remember arriving home, all I remember is Neil standing at the front door, saying good-bye. I was standing up holding Samantha and looking at him puzzled. "Where are you going"? Which is a normal question for a new mom to ask right? "Back to work, what will people think if I stay home"? He answered. I was furious. "People might think less of you for leaving your newborn baby and wife home alone." He didn't seem to agree because he left, and went to work anyway. When I tried to feed her, she continued to gag and throw up whatever went in. I was so scared, hurt, and now so angry. I just stood there holding Samantha, and then something inside me was ignited. That fighter instinct took over, even though the anger stayed. My lesson in life was clear; I had to remain independent. I looked down at Samantha, feeling so scared, and so blessed at the same time. I held her close and I said, "It's okay Samantha, we don't need anybody. I will take care of you, you don't need anybody else". I never realized the impact those words would have until years later.

I also know in my heart, even though I didn't realize it then, that my marriage would never survive that moment. I can be so loving and trusting, but once I'm hurt that deeply, I find it very difficult to regain that love and trust. I was so angry and full of hate that I didn't want to see Neil when he came home at the end of the day or the days that followed. It took me a very long time to forgive him.

There were many days that I would pack up Samantha and leave the house to spend the day with Mimi, or visit Monica and my niece Kelsey. I couldn't spend day after day home alone with my newborn. Neil's parents were extremely kind and helpful. They would come over on the weekends, feeling that Neil worked hard all week, so they didn't want him working hard on the weekend too. While that was so kind of them, I also needed to feel supported during the week, and I needed to feel that I was important too.

Years went on and I had issues over Neil's schedule. He was still enjoying his usual winter sports and lots of summer golfing. I have always been someone who needed a great deal of sleep and a newborn was not conducive to that. I needed Neil to be able to help after I fed Samantha, or at least be around for moral support. We saw things differently. In Neil's mind, because I was breastfeeding, he didn't feel like there was anything he could do.

We do have many good memories as well, with vacations, family time, and friends. The next best day of my life happened fifteen months after Samantha was born, when I found out I was pregnant with Sydney. Once again my sister was also pregnant, which was great and it meant our kids would be close in age. Neil and I were happy, although something deep inside me had never quite recovered. Sydney was born on July 16, 1994, she didn't give me as much of a hard time coming into the world. I had been smart enough this time to plan ahead and had asked Neil to take time off from work. He was able to take a few days off, and then go to work late for a week or so, which was an improvement. He grew up with a very strong work ethic, which I'm not critical of, but I do feel there are times in life when family should come first. I never felt as though we came first.

The second day home with Sydney, Neil went golfing. Then he was planning to golf the entire upcoming weekend. At first I was sucked into trying to organize the two kids, until I lost it, realizing that we should be the priority. Once again we were fighting about his golf and my misery came back. Somehow I gathered the strength to move past this and work on being a happy family. I wanted my own family so badly, that I pushed my frustration aside. I had two beautiful daughters and my husband was a good guy. I had what I wanted, so I needed to learn to be happy.

Heartbreaking Decisions: 1997–1999

A FEW YEARS PASSED, AND I felt as though I was always trying to be happy, while never really feeling happy. I loved being a mom, and I felt so blessed to have my two beautiful daughters. I wanted to give them everything I didn't have. I loved them with all my heart and soul. I often felt angry but I didn't understand why. Neil tried to help by always encouraging me to go out with friends. He even suggested that I join a soccer team, so I did. I found a great group of friends, and very much enjoyed the time I spent with them. Although I had this outlet, I began to feel as though Neil and I were not living as a couple.

I felt I should see a psychologist to resolve issues from my childhood. As I went through sessions, the childhood issues didn't seem to matter. When the psychologist asked me what I loved most about my husband I looked at her and froze. It was like she asked me a question about nuclear physics. I could not answer. The longer it took the more panicked I became, and then it hit me. It was my marriage that was making me so angry and unhappy. I remembered telling my sister how all I ever wanted was to be married and have a family, yet I was miserable.

After months of seeing a psychologist, the time came when I had to make the hardest decision of my life. My head was trying to convince me to stick with it, but my heart knew that I needed to end my marriage. We tried therapy together, but it didn't do anything for me. It made me more frustrated, because I felt like I was giving Neil hope, when I knew there was none. Six month passed and we were living more like roommates than husband and wife. As long as we were not arguing Neil felt as though things were getting better, but they were not. It was truly the most difficult time in my life.

One day when Neil was at work and the kids were at school, Neil's parents came to talk to me. It was heart-breaking, and made me feel horrible. They asked why I was doing this, why I was breaking up a marriage when Neil was a good guy, he didn't drink, or abuse me. They were right on every count, but through my tears I tried to explain how I just did not love him anymore. If I stayed I wouldn't survive, and the kids would be left without a mother. Given my past, they felt that I could never be happy. I couldn't bear it anymore, I ran out of the kitchen sobbing. Neil's dad followed me and kept talking, but I couldn't handle anymore. I was hurting them, hurting Neil, the kids, but I was in pain too. I felt as though nobody seemed to care about that, except for Mimi and Helen.

Mimi and Helen stood by me. Mimi continued to give me the love and support I needed, but I was always careful because she worried about me so much. We had such a strong bond, that if I was hurt, she was hurt. There were times I had to protect her from my pain, so I would put on a brave face, and just give her the facts. I saved the crying for when I was home alone.

Through everything I had ever been through, this had to be the worst. There were times I would imagine being in a coma just to be free of all of this. No, I didn't contemplate how to put myself in a coma, I just wanted to be numb, free of all the pain. Then I did what I knew best; counted the blessings I did have, and got ready to deal with what was ahead. I had my two beautiful daughters, and I had to be strong for them. I had to fight through this to keep them safe and happy. They were my life.

Long ago, I had learned to disconnect from sadness. I didn't even realize it, but it was how I learned to cope. Stay distracted, disconnect from the pain and get through difficult times. I was having a great time with my soccer friends. They were a great group of people and we accepted each other for who we were. Then I met someone in this group. Although Barry turned out to be a total ass, he kept me distracted while my life was in a shambles. Neil was not moving out, and I felt like we were roommates who barely spoke. I was trying to stay sane with this other part of my life. That was how I handled misery. I either disconnect, or I just had fun. Right, wrong, everyone had an opinion. I hid my new relationship from Neil, obviously. To me, our marriage was done and it was a matter of time before he moved out. I had been very blunt on many occasions saying that the marriage was over. I was miserable and now I was being judged and criticized. I thought I had friends, but once again I discovered who my true friends were. Even my sister and I were drifting apart. Everyone picked sides, but nobody seemed to pick my side, except for Mimi and Helen. Even though everyone saw how unhappy I was, and understood how Neil and I were just not meant to be, they did not support me. There were many times that I felt very alone in my life and this was one of them.

Since I was still going out and having fun, it was perceived that this was easy for me. It was often perceived that I was never alone or lonely. I never walked around looking sad or crying, because I had learned long ago that people tend to get sick of that. I hated myself, but I knew I could not live in an unhappy marriage. I carried the guilt for days, months and years.

I moved into an apartment complex nearby our neighborhood with the girls.

It seemed to be the area where all the "divorcees" lived. I had been lucky to find a sublet, a great two-bedroom apartment. The girls shared a bedroom and even had their own bathroom. We lived in this apartment for about eight months. Today, looking back, the girls always tell me how much they loved our time in that apartment.

Our arrangement was based on the girls' needs. At first Samantha struggled a great deal. Anytime she was away from me, she was worried that I was going to die. Samantha always had many unexplained fears. After all I did tell her that she didn't need anybody else and that I would take care of her. I continue to carry so much guilt because of this. Sydney always seemed happy and would go to her dad's or be with me, always smiling, until one day out of the blue, she had a total meltdown. I had dropped the girls off at their dad's and as I was driving away, Sydney came running out of the house screaming and crying. "Why did you get divorced? I hate this, who decided this?" I was shocked and sad all at the same time. There were no words to comfort Sydney. She had kept her feelings hidden until this moment. I held her in my arms while she cried her little heart out. I told her how sorry I was, and how much her dad and I loved her and Samantha. I was so worried about Samantha and Sydney. Every time they were in a strange mood, I thought of how I was ruining their lives. It took a great deal of therapy, and many years before I could let go of the guilt.

Our first Christmas Eve as a separated couple, we still spent together at Neil's parent's. Since every year prior to the divorce Christmas Eve was spent with my sister, and my nieces, I felt it was important this year, to maintain the tradition for the kids and my in-laws.

My relationship with Barry continued, but he had moved to Australia months before. The perception was that I ended my marriage because of Barry, even though I told those who judged that it was not at all the reason. Most people who knew me saw how unhappy I was and understood; others judged and stayed away. I knew Barry was not for me. He was a total womanizer, did not have a solid job or career, and had no direction in his life. He was fun, and we had fun for a while. Barry came to visit and when he did it was always bittersweet. There was a strain with him living so far away and I didn't fully trust him. He would become defensive if I asked questions, which in itself made him look guilty. I became that woman who believed that a womanizer could move across the world and be faithful. I was choosing to believe him.

A few months passed and I was excited to be getting ready to move into a new home. However I was feeling extremely tired, and even though I was often tired, this felt worse. One day while working out with a friend, I turned to her and said, "I am so tired, and I feel like something is sucking all the energy out of me". Then it hit me. I felt panic rise within my gut. It couldn't be, how could I be pregnant? Then I tried to calm down, realizing that there was no way I could be pregnant. It had been months since my last period, but that was nothing new. My mind started racing, I was on the pill, had I missed a pill last time Barry was in town? I had a bad feeling, and all I knew is that I had to get to a pharmacy.

The next morning my friend came over, and waited while I took the test. When I walked out of the bathroom, she knew. She was excited for me, and even congratulated me, but I was not happy. My world was coming down on me once again. I was so angry with myself. How could I be this stupid? I did not want another child, especially not with Barry or with any other man. I had my daughters, and I loved them so much. I wanted to give them all I could, so how could I now start another family? I could not begin to imagine having a child with Barry, sharing this child, knowing he was not a family man. His family would want to have this child, but they were not even that welcoming to me, so I could not imagine any of this working. As these thoughts were screaming in my head all at once, I felt the room spinning, and then I broke down in tears.

I knew I had to tell Barry, even though I knew what he was going to say, and my decision had already been made. When we spoke, as I suspected, his words were cold, "well you aren't going to keep it right"? I told him that as much as it was difficult to think about having an abortion, I felt I had no other choice.

Days later, Barry called again. He was going to come visit, which I thought was nice, but I was paying for his airline ticket. I wasn't sure I wanted him here. We often argued when he came into town, because he was always running off to see his friends or family. It was not a pleasant experience anymore, and I knew this process would be an even more difficult one. I was scared and felt horrible about even wanting to have an abortion.

When Barry did arrive he was in a bad mood, feeling as though this may be his only chance to have a child even though deep down he knew he never wanted to have kids. The whole experience was horrible. He came with me to the clinic, and tried to be supportive. I was numb, emotionless, and totally disconnected from the whole procedure. Afterwards I needed to rest, but he wanted to be doing something else. We compromised and went to see a movie, "Meet Joe Black," which was not the smartest decision. I cried uncontrollably, to the point that Barry got impatient, which only made me more upset. The next day Barry left to go see his family, leaving me feeling very hurt. He traveled all this way to be with me, and was now using this trip as a little vacation. I then told myself it was best if I just stayed on my own to rest. I actually couldn't wait for him to leave to go back to Australia. My heart told me that I shouldn't have involved him, that I should have just done this with the help of a friend.

Months later I moved into a new home with Samantha and Sydney. We were excited to be back in our old neighborhood. The girls and I had so much fun! When the girls were at their dad's, I would have parties or go out with my friends. At this point even Mimi and Helen were trying to get me to stay home more. I didn't see why I should sit at home on my own when I didn't have my kids with me. I was always the type of person who needed life to go on, and find a way to be happy. My soccer friends were a huge part of my life, very supportive, and even though some of them tried to warn me about Barry, I didn't listen.

The following Christmas was very difficult. Barry was in town, but spent most of his time with his family in the country. Christmas Eve arrived and we all went to church. Neil, his parents, his sisters, my sister, my brother-in-law, and my nieces all sat together. We were all in the church, but I wasn't really with them. Samantha and Sydney were singing in the choir, and I was with friends. After mass they all went back to Neil's parents to continue the Christmas Eve tradition. I went home on my own, I didn't want to be that person who cried and got upset, since I now had what I wanted. Even though I was the one who wanted the divorce, it didn't mean it was always easy. When I arrived at home, Barry called. As soon as I heard his voice, my dam burst and I was sobbing. He felt terrible, left his family, and arrived on my doorstep within the hour. This was the kind side of Barry and I was very touched by his actions. We spent the rest of the night together and the next morning he went back to his family. I was eager to spend Christmas day with Samantha, Sydney, Mimi, and Helen.

The long distance relationship continued until I found emails about his excursions and weekends away with other women. Why had I been so stupid? How could I be shocked? It was who he was, a womanizer, a cheater and a liar. He would tell me so many times that I was the only one for him and he loved me so much. I fell for all of it. Now I felt stupid, but when I wanted to break up, he went nuts. He was still in Australia so there was nothing he could do.

Thirty Something: 1997–2004

I SPENT MUCH OF MY THIRTIES worried about my kids, trying to build a normal life. During the years after my divorce Monica and I drifted further apart for different reasons. Unfortunately, that meant that I didn't get to see my nieces very often. I knew that I didn't have any control over the situation, and I learned to accept it. I was happy that the four girls still spent time together and continued to bond as cousins. I set my intention to be close to Kelsey and Jasmine in years to follow. I would close my eyes and imagine them older, feeling in my heart that we would be close. Years later when Kelsey and Jasmine were in high school, my wishes came true. They began to visit and spent a lot of time with us. We have so many amazing memories together, and I am grateful for this.

There were many strange things that happened during the years that followed. I had been hospitalized once again, but this time for a strange ear infection. While away on vacation I perforated my eardrum. I woke up one night with throbbing pain and blood on my pillow. It was so painful and it felt worse because I was not home. I had to find a random doctor to get a prescription for antibiotics. By the time I got back home the pain was worse, and I could not get out of bed without throwing up or falling over. My sister brought me to the hospital, where I stayed for a week until the infection calmed down. I wasn't strong enough to take care of myself, so once I got out of the hospital I stayed with Mimi and

Helen. I was too weak to be home with the girls, but they came to visit me. I had been through a rough time, and as if that wasn't enough, I picked up a voice mail from my gynecologist. The message said it was urgent, and that I had to see him right away. Test results showed pre-cancerous cells in my cervix and I had to have a biopsy immediately.

I have never been someone who worried over health issues or jumped to conclusions. I went for the biopsy and although it wasn't the most pleasant experience, it was a very fast procedure. Everything seemed under control and I was instructed to have a colposcopy every six months to be sure I was in the clear. This is very common for many women. For me, I knew I needed to change my diet and figure out why my body was plagued by weird infections.

I realized that I was trying to suppress a great deal of anger. I was angry about my childhood, starting to realize that it was in fact a big deal. I realized that I was angry with my mom for just letting herself die, and I was also angry that my marriage didn't work out. Anger is such a powerful emotion, but I never realized how much was inside of me. How could there not be?

I was still yearning to have a family, which must have made me visibly vulnerable because I met John, who persistently pursued me. Even though at first I thought I had made it clear that I was not interested in a relationship with him. John helped with my hip injury, I trusted his ability and was very appreciative of his help. I had been injured from a water skiing accident and had a great deal of trouble getting the proper treatment. I had been unable to walk or stand for more than ten minutes at a time, without resting to relieve some pain. John helped me and also put me in contact with the right people for orthodics. These inserts for my shoes, combined with treatments, eliminated my pain. I was able to get back to my soccer games and working out.

John also knew a doctor who was willing to see me as a new patient. I had spent years trying to find a doctor of my own, so I was very relieved that I no longer had to run to a clinic to see random doctors. For years I had been dealing with extreme fatigue. Doctors kept trying to put me on anti-depressants. They couldn't figure out why I could not get through a day without napping. They insisted my thyroid levels were fine, so they tested for other autoimmune disorders. They couldn't find any answers, so they kept insisting that I was depressed. I was criticized many times over the years for needing so much sleep, but that was who I was, or so I thought. John finally asked my new doctor to check my thyroid antibodies. The doctor called me personally to tell me that my antibodies were quite high, even though my other thyroid levels were within normal range. He was not at all surprised that I couldn't stay awake. After a few weeks of being on medication, I could finally get through a day without sleeping. It was such a relief. Obviously I was feeling very grateful to John.

He courted me and literally got down on one knee on one of our first dates. Now I was really confused because I was not in love but I was in awe, probably dealing with transference of feelings. John helped me through a very difficult time, and after years of suffering, I was getting answers. John was persistent and I started wondering if I wasn't always picking the wrong type of man, maybe John was different. So not long after we began to date, we decided to try living together. I was worried about Samantha and Sydney, but they didn't seem unhappy with the arrangement. They were the most important people in my life. Even though many people were warning me not to be with John, I didn't listen. My sister was not at all happy because she didn't trust him, putting an added strain on our relationship.

Before I met John, I was living happily in my home with my daughters. I didn't have any debt and life was stress free financially. I was so vulnerable that I couldn't see what was happening clearly. John wanted to buy a bigger home. He was quite successful so I felt confident that taking out a mortgage would be fine. I had told him that since I had set myself up to stay at home while my kids were young, that I couldn't afford a mortgage. If things didn't work out, I would not be in a good position. He assured me, the mortgage would be paid off quickly…

John and I got married in Barbados in 2002. My instincts were against this, but for some reason I was pulled toward this life. Once married, there were times when I discovered John was lying about things that didn't make sense. My inner voice was sending warning signals, but I was trying to ignore the signs, feeling that I couldn't imagine getting divorced again. Time passed, years passed, things were getting worse, and I was constantly getting sick.

John recommended I meet Anne-Marie, a Holistic Naturopath, for my intestinal problems. Years before I had been diagnosed with irritable bowel syndrome, but was never really told how I could treat it. Since Anne-Marie treats the body as a whole, she looks at all of the factors that influence our health. Her approach in Natural Health examines emotions, how we think, cultural inheritance, and the impact of stress on physical health. The key is to restore balance, while following the belief that our body has the capacity to heal itself.

Anne-Marie is one of the most beautiful souls on this earth. She has a beautiful, and loving smile. Her warmth and beauty shine right through her angelic being. Not only did I feel immediately at ease, but also I trusted her opinion. Even though I always loved to eat my fruits and vegetables, I was also addicted to junk food. Anne-Marie helped me create a much healthier lifestyle. This was a defining moment, making me realize that I needed to fuel my body with much healthier foods.

Anne-Marie also began helping me on a very different level, an energetic one. Think about it, you are energy. Each one of you has an energy field surrounding you. When there is a full moon, statistics show that emergency rooms are busier; there are more accidents, and a higher rate of crime. These are real statistics, which prove how much we are affected by the energies around us. Have you ever noticed having a more emotional reaction to something when there is a full moon? Have you ever had a strange fight that escalates out of nothing, only to realize there had been a full moon?

Anne-Marie's energy sessions are a very powerful form of therapy. Healing not only on a physical level, but also an energetic level has been an integral part of self-empowerment and evolution for me. Many of you may be resistant to energy work since it's something the human eye cannot see. Some people possess the unique gift to see beyond the physical self, which is something Anne-Marie can do. I like to think of energy work as a "work out" not just on our physical body, but also on a much deeper level, our energetic self.

Imagine a screen door protecting your home from dirt and sand, only allowing the breeze of the warm summer air to come in. If the weather begins to change and the winds grew stronger, the screen would not be able to protect your home as much, allowing extra dirt to blow in. Now imagine what would happen if a sudden storm came through and the screen ripped; much more dirt, tree branches, bugs, and wind would be howling in, creating a much bigger mess.

Our human body, and energy field are similar to this. Think about walking into a room filled with people. Can you feel when a room is filled with positive or negative energy? With the positive energy you feel light and inspired, whereas with negative energy you feel drained and tired. That energy gets into your field and affects how you feel. It's like meeting someone and immediately having a good feeling versus a bad feeling. Think about times when you don't want to be around certain negative people, whereas you are drawn to other positive people. If life situations occur that create a great deal of negativity, this makes our energy field weak, leaving us less capable of fending off other forms of negativity. If something even more tragic occurs, a death, loss of a job, or divorce, your field becomes even weaker, creating little "holes" in the field around you. This can create a feeling of not being fully present in your own body. Some of you may have experienced that feeling of "being there, but not really being there." You can walk around and talk to people, but you feel too down or weak to be fully present.

Anne-Marie has helped me work through difficult past experiences in order to strengthen my field. Acting as a translator, Anne-Marie is able to identify emotions within my conscious or subconscious. Her sessions begin with a verbal conversation and as we move into the energy session, Anne-Marie helps me release negative emotions, which may be creating blockages. As I am comfortably lying down, Anne-Marie helps to clear and repair my energy field through very graceful hand movements over my body.

As I was working with Anne-Marie something inside me was changing. I was becoming more aware of the truth. During these years with John, I had one infection after the other. First it was my finger that had a small blister, which turned into an infection that almost caused the doctors to cut it off. Then I had a cyst on my buttocks that went so deep that I ended up in the emergency room. The plastic surgeon on call began to literally cut away at my buttocks, asking me why I wasn't feeling anything. Luckily I wasn't, because she had to cut a very large hole to clear the infection.

The doctor was convinced that I was either on drugs or being abused. I had cysts in my arms and both sides of my buttocks. These are also common injection sites, which is what triggered her suspicion. I told her to test my blood because it would be clear that I was not a drug user. She could tell I was hiding something… I just didn't want to admit that I was letting my husband inject me with antibiotics. Through my tears I begged her to just let it go, and after a few visits, she agreed. I just needed to heal, which took months of daily visits to the clinic to "pack" my open wound until it healed. Since John told me he was a nurse, I assumed he could help with cleaning the wound while we were away on vacation. When I had to explain the procedure to him I began to question the validity of his claims. This whole experience began to open my eyes to the real man I had married.

I was now waking up and the next few months became a blur because of what I was to discover. I had been blind. I was about to have one of my most powerful energy sessions with Anne-Marie. One day in May 2005, Anne-Marie released something on a much deeper level. The healing takes time because it is like peeling an onion. First working at surface level, and as each layer is peeled away, more is seen which allows for deeper emotions to be released. As Anne-Marie works, things are revealed to her. She lifted an important part of what was shielding me from seeing the truth. I had been living in a hologram. It was my key to survival as a young child. It was as though I was living outside my own body, unable to see things clearly. The traumatic events were too difficult, so this was my way of protecting myself. It was as though I could never see things clearly because I had buried events so deeply within myself in order to survive.

I can't begin to explain how powerful this one session was. It was as though for so many years I had been living in a fog. Now that the fog had lifted, I could see things clearly for the first time. When John asked how my session was, I told him to sit down. Then without hesitation I told him our marriage was over. We were done, and I wanted him out. There was no wavering on my part. I was now capable of seeing the truth, the truth that was begging to be seen. He was not who he claimed to be. I walked around in disbelief for weeks. I was numb. How did I not see it? How did I even end up with him? Then again, it was part of something I had to experience and live in this life.

Many people tried to warn me not to be with him, that he wasn't for me. I didn't listen. Friends sometimes want to control you and make your decisions, because to them, it's all so clear. This goes beyond, "you can't see the forest from the trees". A friend may offer advice and express things that may not be obvious to you due to your proximity to the situation. I was already feeling bad enough without people saying, "I told you so". I was living my life and clearly making mistakes, and I felt it was unnecessary for anyone to make me feel even worse by stating the obvious.

I feel like the fact that John, being an older man, who promised to take care of me, was what I needed at the time. I had been with John for over five years, married for almost four of the years, and now was going through a difficult time realizing I felt trapped and stupid. I knew at this point, that he was not at all who he claimed to be. There were many lies. He told me that he had been married once before when in fact he had been married twice. He had convinced me that he had cancer years before, but that was a lie too. He told me he was a nurse, another lie. He had put tens of thousands of dollars on my credit cards. Life was a mess. He got me deeper and deeper into debt. I believe that he wasn't being true to himself. He really wasn't a family man but was trying to live this ideal role, maybe because of societal pressures. I don't know but part of that pressure came from him wanting a family for his two kids when they would come to visit at Christmas or in the summer. It was as though he was trying to force his life into something that was just not for him. I finally woke up, thanks to Anne-Marie's intervention, and my willingness to finally see the truth.

To this day people still make jokes in a conversation about my multiple marriages. It used to bother me, but now I laugh at myself. I know they aren't trying to be hurtful, but that was part of my struggle to end my second marriage. I kept thinking about how many people would gossip and once again I would be judged. How could I be that woman who was divorced twice? What about my kids? They would now have a mom who had two broken marriages. What kind of an example is that? Then I realized it didn't matter because I have a good life, actually, I have a great life. I have shown my daughters how to be courageous and to not settle for unhappiness even if it is difficult to make the necessary changes. What kind of lesson would it be for them if I had stayed with someone like John? I left their father Neil because I was unhappy, so I certainly was not going to stay with anyone else. I always gave my daughters love and stability within the instability. The one thing I always made sure of was that any man in my life, was good to my daughters. They were sad when John and I separated, but once I explained why, they understood. The most important thing was that the three of us were together.

"Food For Thought"

M Y FORTIES STARTED WITH THE ending of my second marriage and learning more about myself. Very quickly I found myself in a new relationship with Timothy. Sometimes life just happens and even though we were both fresh out of our marriages, something just clicked. This was something that I jumped into, following my heart.

Samantha and Sydney were now in high school and it was time for me to start working again. This was a difficult time as many things were changing. I was still recovering from the last marriage, in a new relationship, and I had to find a new career. I knew I wanted to help people, have a flexible schedule and be passionate about what I was doing. During the few years prior I had been receiving a type of massage called Lymphatic Drainage. This is a very gentle technique which helps improve lymphatic flow and helps the immune system. I had done this because my lymph nodes in my neck were always swollen, probably due to all the infections that had plagued me over the years. As I was receiving these treatments, and because they were so beneficial to me, I had entertained the idea of becoming a therapist. My first step was to take Massage Therapy courses, so I nervously enrolled, once again following my heart.

Being back in school was interesting. There were two situations, which took me by surprise, and made me realize that there were clearly some issues I still needed to deal with. The first situation was during the practical lessons where we had to perform the techniques we just learned. I had to partner up with a male, which created panic to rise within me. I quickly managed to switch partners, which was a clear indication that I had more to deal with regarding the sexual abuse. Now wasn't the time, and I couldn't let what I was feeling interfere with the pursuit of my new career. I questioned whether I would be able to massage men at all and wondered if it was feasible to build a business massaging only women. Through some therapy and more energy work, I managed to release these fears and have successfully built a massage business working comfortably with any gender.

The second time I reacted was when we were asked to take a long piece of brown paper and draw an outline of our own body. I just froze. I didn't understand why, but I couldn't move. I could not draw myself and my emotions were beginning to choke me. I began to cry, and then sob. The teacher took me aside, and through the conversation it became clear that I had to deal with my issues of low self-esteem and a negative body image.

I have always had a negative image of myself but now it seemed heightened, as once again I was feeling even more vulnerable. I have tried very hard to work through this and not find fault every time I look in the mirror. It's an ongoing process, which at times can be difficult. Society has given all of us a challenge. Magazine covers often contain photos of beautiful and extremely fit women, with headings about dieting or losing ten pounds. It's not just the women anymore, men also have the added pressure to look a certain way. Yes we all want to look our best, but the emphasis that is placed on that perfect body can become overwhelming. So many women and men deal with these issues. Many of you may be very critical of yourself, but I have realized as many of you may feel, that we are often our own worst critics.

I've never really had a weight problem, but my perception was that I did. I have been obsessed with losing weight since I was a teen. Anyone who really knows me has heard me talk about the need to lose ten pounds. In high school I weighed around 116 pounds, which is a perfect weight for someone my height (5'4") at that age. But I always felt the need to lose ten pounds.

I feel fortunate that I never suffered from bulimia or anorexia but binge eating is one of many eating disorders. Binge eating was something that I did for many years but never talked about or had diagnosed. I also never quite realized I was a binge eater until later in life when I started studying nutrition.

I came to realize that I had been on a cycle of dieting and binging since high school. The cycle continued for many years. I could literally start eating chips, then chocolate, ice cream, licorice, candy, and then popsicles, all in one evening. Of course after my binge, I felt terrible both physically and mentally. The feelings of guilt were overwhelming and I hated myself for doing it. It seemed to become a form of self-abuse. Anytime I was at the point when I felt really good about myself, my eating behavior would change for the worse and I would binge, beginning the cycle over again. Throughout the years I searched for answers as to why I always had some form of stomach pain. Even at times when I was eating normally, the pain was there. I have learned so much about myself while trying to change my way of thinking, to fix my digestive problems, my joint pain and all my other annoying symptoms. Even though Anne-Marie had helped me to feel much better, there was still something that did not feel quite right.

I had omitted dairy many years before, but I had been enjoying soymilk and was somewhat resistant to that change. One spring I was following a detox program and eliminated common triggers for digestive issues (flour, corn, dairy, sugar, alcohol) except for my coffee and soymilk. I had a rash at the base of my neck that had been there for almost ten years. I had been to doctors and dermatologists, who prescribed creams that burned through me, but never helped my rash. It was at the point where I was scratching in my sleep, I would wake up to find my neck bleeding. As I began this cleanse, my rash seemed to get worse. I realized that I had to eliminate the soymilk. After ten years with this rash, it was gone within four days of eliminating the soymilk. This was a huge relief, and made me realize how many people may be suffering from certain skin conditions because of a food intolerance.

Many months passed and my intestinal issues got worse again. I never felt quite well enough. The next piece of the puzzle was found when I met a blood specialist who tested for food intolerances, a subject that intrigued me. Twenty years prior I had tested positive for fructose and sorbitol intolerance. Other than a lactose test, there was never an option to test for anything else. I immediately made an appointment to have the blood test done. The results showed a long list of food intolerances, which included gluten, dairy, sugar cane, soy, and bananas. No wonder I didn't feel well!

I would never recommend eliminating food groups without the proper testing. In my opinion food intolerances may be contributing to specific health issues that are becoming more prominent in today's society. Lack of proper nutrition and/or food intolerances can have a strong affect on issues such as; poor digestion, skin irritations, irritability, difficulty concentrating, insomnia, to name a few. There are so many books on the market with different information regarding food for blood types, anti-inflammation diets, healing with whole foods, etc. The key is to find the right answers for you, because we are all unique.

My daughter Samantha finally agreed to be tested for food intolerances. She has suffered with facial cysts, which were often misdiagnosed as acne. She would get big sores that were extremely painful and obviously unpleasant. Her test results showed intolerances to gluten and dairy. Once she eliminated both, she no longer got the cysts. In moments of weakness, when she has dairy, smaller versions of the cysts, sometimes come back.

A gluten intolerance is extremely different to celiac disease, since celiac is an allergy to gluten it can actually damage the intestines. If testing for celiac comes up negative, I would highly recommend being tested for gluten intolerance. Many people get tested for celiac and when the result is negative, the assumption is, that they don't have a problem with gluten. That was what happened to me, yet I knew gluten made me feel sick and created many problems. As it turns out, my test for gluten intolerance showed a positive result. I may not have had celiac disease, but I was gluten intolerant.

Being gluten intolerant is not a fad, although some may think it is. Gluten intolerance can create many different issues. For me, gluten will affect my skin, my digestion and even my mood. I can become irritable and extremely tired if I eat gluten for consecutive days. Having eliminated it for many months, I am able to have small amounts of gluten infrequently. Gluten intolerance versus a gluten allergy may create different symptoms for many different people, so I feel proper testing is the key.

Our bodies and brains need fuel, proper fuel. Would you ever consider using anything other than gasoline to fuel your gas-powered car? It wouldn't last very long if you did…so why don't we treat our bodies the same way? Our moods, our skin, our digestion are all greatly affected by foods we eat, especially for someone like me, who does have food intolerances. This is just some "food for thought".

Happily Ever After

For Timothy and I, our situation was literally a disaster waiting to happen. Together we had four kids. Samantha and Sydney were 13 and 11, and Kendall and TJ were 13 and 18. The girls already knew each other from playing hockey together, so their bonding continued. Since TJ was older, it was different for him, and in some ways more difficult. Somehow we all made it through, even though Timothy and I had no idea what we were doing. Neither one of us knew what we were getting into, nor did we behave or think like adults. We both just jumped in!

Only months into our relationship, we decided to take our first trip together with our three daughters. We drove fourteen hours to Virginia Beach. I thought somebody was going to be left behind and it very well could have been me. All three girls were going through their own adjustments. At times they were having fun, but most of the time somebody was upset, crying, or pissed off.

From the time Kendall was a young kid, her summers were spent at the city pool with her friends. She was on the waterpolo team, competed on the swim team, and practiced all summer for the final synchronized swimming competition. Timothy and I made the brilliant decision to leave on our vacation during the summer. Not only was she away from all of that, but she was also missing her mom. We were obviously not thinking clearly. I think we just wanted to be on our own to bond with the three girls, but it almost backfired.

Samantha had this huge fear of me dying, so anytime I went away even for the day, she would get extremely upset. The trip was already filled with every kind of emotion, but I thought it was a great time to tell Samantha that I was leaving to go to Florida for a week-long continuing education class only a few days after we were due to return from Virginia. Samantha spent the rest of the trip sad, crying, or hanging on to me. Sydney spent most of the time in the room, escaping all of us, enjoying her time alone watching the Disney channel. This wasn't how I wanted our vacation to be spent. I wanted to cut the trip short and just go home, but we stuck it out. Despite the many difficult moments and the awful drive home, we did manage to have some fun and laughs. At this point Timothy and I weren't sure that we would make it as a couple, or ever take another vacation together. Our bond was already strong, and once home we happily continued our relationship.

On top of all the struggles of blending a family, like learning how to co-parent, we also had the normal challenges of a new relationship. Timothy and I began living together, but we had to sell the house and downsize, even though the house I was living in was a better size for all of us, the taxes and mortgage were too much for us to handle. I was taking courses for Massage Therapy, and needed to start working as soon as possible. There were many obstacles along the way. Had we both looked for the easy way out, we would not be living the amazing life we are enjoying together today.

I know how much Timothy loves and adores me, and I feel same way. But somehow I had not been communicating this to him. Totally unaware, that after my years of broken relationships, I had become afraid to really give myself to Timothy. One day I was listening to Josh Groban's song "You Raise Me Up". As I listened to the words, I was thinking of how much I loved Timothy, and how much he supported me in every aspect of my life. The tears began to flow and I was overwhelmed with emotion. The realization of how much I needed him and how much he gave me strength suddenly overwhelmed me. I also realized that I was allowed to feel as though I needed someone. It wasn't until this moment that I truly realized how much I always tried to be independent, and because of this, my love for Timothy was not properly projected. As much as I thought I was showing Timothy how much I loved him, I was also holding back. My epiphany only brought us closer together.

I had been told in some relationships that I was needy. I knew I wasn't, I just wanted to feel loved. When someone tells you that, the underlying message is that they can't give you what you want or deserve. Believe in love and believe that you deserve to be loved regardless of past experiences.

Timothy and I were married in Orlando, Florida August 2008 with Samantha, Sydney, and Kendall. Since it was my third marriage and Timothy's second, we decided to make this a very quiet and personal ceremony on the beach. Our relationship has blossomed over the years as we continue to learn more about ourselves, and each other. Through each obstacle, our family has only grown closer. We have been on many family trips together since our first disastrous trip, and have always had an amazing time. It was our special time together, without the girls having to go back and forth between homes. I always felt so happy being together as a family. Our Disney trips have been the best part of our family vacations. One of the very best trips was in 2011 when we met my nieces Kelsey, Jasmine, and their Dad at Walt Disney World. We had a day filled with rides and lots of laughs. It was so amazing, and filled my heart with so much love and joy.

For so many years, holidays never felt quite right. Timothy and I never wanted the kids to feel pulled in too many directions, even though divorce is a situation that can create that feeling. We always encourage the kids to make plans with their other parents first, to avoid problems. For years we never even planned a Christmas dinner. In December 2013, I decided to plan a Christmas dinner one weekend early. As I sat around seeing all of us together; Timothy and I with our four kids, boyfriends, girlfriends, Helen, my sister, and my nieces all in one room, my heart was filled with so much gratitude, love, and joy. I finally had the family I always wanted. Timothy and I now have our own family tradition for Christmas.

I feel so blessed that I am so in love and happily married for, yes, my third time. Had I given up, I would be missing out on such a great part of my life. Timothy had been warned by some people not to be with me. Once again people's perception of me was wrong. Since I had been married twice, the perception was that I just toss men aside, and that made me so sad. Timothy did not allow these negative perceptions to cloud his judgment. He followed his heart, trusting in his own instinct, and the love we felt for each other. Timothy is the funniest and most amazing man ever. His smile is infectious. His sense of humor, warmth, support, and unconditional love, overwhelms me at times. I feel truly proud and blessed to call him my husband. I am very happy that I never gave up on love.

Mimi

THROUGH ALL THE CHANGES THAT were going on in my life, Mimi was also enduring changes. She was having a difficult time moving around on her own and seemed to be in more pain as each day passed. Mimi had a hard life and it wasn't getting any easier. Mimi suffered from angina and from osteo-arthritis, which was becoming debilitating for her. It was heart breaking for the rest of us because Mimi was such a strong, vibrant woman with so much life left in her and the will to do so much more. Her pain was becoming intolerable. On some days she had trouble walking, and on other days she couldn't move her arms. It got to the point where she couldn't get herself dressed. Before leaving for work, Helen would have to wake Mimi up to help her wash up and get changed.

I visited Mimi often, just spending an afternoon with her, or helping her do groceries and run errands. We had a great time together, always able to talk about anything. She knew everything about my life and loved me unconditionally. Mimi was my best friend, she took such good care of me throughout my life, and now it was my turn to take care of her. Mimi also had so much trouble hearing over the years. If ever we were shopping and a sales person became impatient with her because she couldn't hear, it would hurt me so much I would become like a bear protecting their cub!

At the age of 89 the decision was made to move Mimi into a home. She had been living with Helen all these years, but it was becoming too hard on Helen and also a concern to leave Mimi alone. Moving Mimi into a home was a difficult decision for the family. As much as Mimi did not want to leave her home, she knew there was no choice. I will never forget the day Shirley, Helen and I brought Mimi to her new home. We walked through the doors and I could tell Mimi was sad and scared. She was so brave and even though she knew this was for the best, this was breaking her heart. I kept talking to Mimi, trying to keep the mood upbeat. I could feel her sadness and I could see the expression on her face. It felt as though we were in an upscale hospital. We walked down the hall, where a nurse greeted us. We were being escorted to Mimi's room, passing opened doors, seeing some familiar faces of people my parents and Mimi knew when I was a kid. How sad I thought, my parents were long gone, and this is where some of the others have ended up. All I thought was how I better just die in my sleep, or have a better place to live if I can't live on my own. I would never want to live with my kids, or become a burden, that is for sure. This is one of many great reasons to create total financial freedom and abundance.

When we arrived at Mimi's room we waited as the nurse unlocked the door. My heart was beating a mile a minute and I stayed very close to Mimi. I wanted to grab her and run away. The door opened leading us into a nice enough room. It was a spacious room with a single bed, and her own sink. Mimi walked in with her walker, sat down in it facing her bed, and with tears in her eyes, said "well this is the last stop for me" and then she burst into tears.

I held onto her for dear life and we were both crying. The nurse tapped me and motioned for me to go outside. I was not happy about that. Shirley and Helen remained composed talking to Mimi, but I could not stop crying, so I went into the hallway. I was crying even harder, but quietly. My heart was breaking into a million pieces. Then I wanted to punch the nurse as she looked at me and asked, "are you the one staying"? I have no idea how I remained standing where I was, because all I wanted to do was lunge forward and grab her by the neck. We were definitely not going to be friends. How could she possibly understand? Mimi was everything to me. She was my world. I wanted to take care of her and couldn't. Adding insult to injury, Mimi was right, this was her last stop.

Mimi was very brave, but this home made her depressed. I tried my best to visit her as often as possible. I loved spending time with her, sharing anything and everything. Mimi knew everything about me, and loved me unconditionally. Our relationship was unique. I always felt that I could be myself with Mimi and never be judged. I respected her so much and never once raised my voice to her. I will never forget the time in my late teens when I was self absorbed and had not called Mimi for days, maybe even longer. When I finally did call her, she told me that she was hurt and wanted to hear from me more often. It broke my heart and from that day forward, I called her almost every day.

Mimi just wanted me to find a "good man". When she met Timothy, she told me to hang on to him, that he was a great guy. One of the many beautiful things about Mimi was that even if she saw a flaw in any man I was with, as long as I was happy, she was happy. With Timothy, there was something different. She knew that he was the one. So did I.

Timothy and I were in a great routine. Every spring break we brought the girls on a trip to Orlando, and even the years we said we wouldn't go to Disney, we usually ended up there anyway. Timothy and I also started a ritual of travelling in November every year. We would arrive in Florida for the American Thanksgiving, and would enjoy the sales while shopping for Christmas. It was always a blast. For Mimi, it was difficult. Every time I left, she would feel lonely. As years went on she couldn't talk on the phone because her hearing had diminished considerably. We tried different hearing aids but nothing helped. Not being able to call her from Florida made it all the more difficult.

At the end of 2008, Timothy's Dad got sick and was displaying the onset of Alzheimer's. Timothy would speak to his Dad several times a day, helping him, talking him through everything. It was time to get outside help. His mom was already in a home, suffering from Alzheimer's and Dementia. Timothy is an amazing man and seeing his devotion and love for his parents warmed my heart. It was a very rough year and in January of 2009 Timothy's dad was hospitalized. Timothy would spend consecutive days keeping him company, helping him with basic hygiene, like shaving. He left the hospital while his dad went for a lung test. The doctors assured Timothy that it would be a simple procedure to check if there was a tumor. During one of their conversations, Timothy's dad told him, that his brother, who had already passed away, was coming for him. That evening, the hospital called to say that his father passed away. Timothy was devastated and shocked. The doctors were unsure of the cause.

The only bright side of Alzheimer's is that his mom didn't suffer the loss of her husband of 50 years. When we went to visit her, she would ask me not to sit on a certain chair because her husband was sitting there. That was sad and comforting all at the same time. Six months later, his mom took a turn for the worse. Her health was declining rapidly and now she had gone blind. June 2009, she passed away to join her husband. Soul mates stay together. Timothy lost both his parents within 5 months, which was heart breaking.

A few months later I had a horrible and vivid nightmare that Mimi died. It was so real. I was sobbing uncontrollably and all I kept saying in my dream is that I had not baked cheese bread with Mimi. I woke up with a heavy heart, and in a panic wanting to see Mimi immediately to plan our next baking date. Our cheese bread is like mini pizza, it's a Lebanese tradition and Mimi's recipe was the best. Mimi was the best cook in the world. Although the process to make the cheese bread was long, it was always a great way for Mimi and me to spend the day together. We used to bake together in her home when the girls were little. Now that

Mimi didn't live in her own apartment anymore, we baked at my home. I would prepare everything the night before, leaving the dough to rise over night. The cheese mixture was prepared as well and our day of baking would begin. Immediately after that horrible nightmare I went to visit Mimi and quickly planned our day to bake.

That November, Timothy and I went on a much needed vacation. It had been a rough year, especially for Timothy after having lost both his parents. I went to visit Mimi the day before we left to Florida, except this time I didn't tell her we were going. I just told her a little white lie saying that I had a really busy week coming up, so not to worry if I didn't come visit. I would be sure to come visit her as soon as things slowed down. She probably knew I was lying, but to me it was better than seeing her so sad knowing I was leaving.

Timothy and I left for Florida the next day. Three days into the trip, we were on the beach when my cell phone rang. I don't even know why I had my cell phone on the beach, because even though we kept in touch with the girls, we kept our phones in our room. I had an unsettling feeling. I missed a call from Shirley. Her message was for me to call her, and I immediately panicked. Timothy tried to reassure me that she probably forgot I was in Florida. Nonetheless I couldn't wait and called her right away.

My instincts were correct. Shirley had taken Mimi to the hospital. She had some bleeding and they needed to do some tests. I was told not to worry, but of course I hung up and burst into tears. I walked down towards the ocean and prayed. I was breathing in the beautiful ocean air, feeling the hot sun against my tense body, trying to calm myself. I just wanted to feel something, but I could feel myself drifting away. I was trying so hard to remain calm, but my inner voice was telling me that this was it, my fears were coming true. Mimi's days were numbered, and I knew that soon she would not live forever. I wanted to be home, even though we still had five days left of our trip. Normally it never seemed long enough, but this time, five days felt like an eternity. I was trying to be considerate of how Timothy was feeling and how much he needed this time away. So I needed to know exactly what was happening with Mimi before making any decisions.

Every morning and evening I spoke with Shirley or Helen. The news sounded good; Mimi had colitis, that I could live with. I had a feeling I was being lied to, but they reassured me that they wouldn't lie to me with something like this. They were worried about me, knowing I was on vacation wanting me to rest and enjoy the trip. No matter how busy I was, Mimi knew I would've been there by her bedside so I asked Shirley to let Mimi know that I was in Florida. Shirley gave me strict instructions from Mimi, to relax and enjoy myself with Timothy and she would see us when we got home. I felt a bit better knowing that Mimi seemed to be okay.

We arrived home Saturday and went to the hospital with the five girls, Samantha, Sydney, Kendall, Kelsey, and Jasmine. We all walked into the room and what we saw was not what we had expected. Mimi was having trouble breathing, she had an oxygen tank next to her and was extremely agitated. Although Mimi was still pleasant with us as we walked in, I knew better, so I signaled to the girls and went out to the waiting room. We had our "crying fest", then I pulled myself together and went back into Mimi's room. Her daughter-in-law Joy was trying to help her get comfortable. The scene was horrific. Joy was having so much trouble just trying to help Mimi lie down. Mimi suddenly seemed as though she had aged twenty years. She always looked much younger than her age, until now. I stayed with her for a little bit, but we all had to rotate our visits. While I was with her, I held her hand in mine. She worked so hard with them and yet they were always so soft. I could tell she was tired and needed to rest. It was so hard seeing her like this. Even at this point she was worried about me, telling me to spend time with the girls the next day, that she would have her kids around her and not to worry.

Monday I dropped the girls off at school and headed straight to the hospital. I couldn't wait to see Mimi. I planned to spend the day with her, until it was time to pick up the girls from school. Once I walked closer to the room I could hear Mimi moaning. As I turned the corner into her room, I couldn't believe my eyes. She was sitting in a chair with tubes in her nose, moaning. The gentleman in the bed next to her said that she was calling for help all night. She was having a lot of trouble breathing and the staff just left her alone for a good part of the night. They had put her in chair and gave her oxygen, she had been sitting there for hours, and just wanted to get back into bed. I was fuming. I didn't want to leave the room, but I had no choice. It took hours before the nurses finally moved her to a room closer to the nurses' station. They could have moved her *into* the nurses' station, for all the good that would do. I didn't care, there was no way that I was going to leave her alone at night anymore! I told Mimi that she was stuck with me sleeping at the hospital with her. She barely argued.

The emotional roller coaster began. That afternoon, I waited for Shirley to arrive before leaving. Mimi was much better and had instructed me to go home to see the kids and come back after dinner. Off I went, feeling a little better. Christmas was fast approaching and I always felt it was important to keep life as up-beat and happy as possible no matter what was going on. I needed to run a few errands. While I was in a store, my phone rang. It was Shirley and she sounded frantic. "Get back right away! Something happened and they aren't sure how much longer she will last".

I called Timothy to hurry home, because I couldn't drive. I was freaking out panicking and wanted to leave right away. What was I thinking? I couldn't wait for Timothy to get home, I had to jump in a taxi to get back to Mimi. Then my phone rang again, my heart almost stopped, but Shirley sounded so much lighter, because now Mimi was fine. There seemed to be a bit of a scare with her heart and her breathing, but the scare was over. Great news, but my inner voice was telling me something else. Once we arrived, Mimi was thrilled to see me. She seemed better than I had imagined, except that now, Mimi had a tube in her neck.

At the end of the evening the family had left and I was given a reclining chair to sleep in. I had some blankets, my sweat pants and sweatshirt and was so happy to be spending the night. I tucked Mimi in, and told her I would be close by if she needed anything at all. I made sure to position my chair so that I was out of the way for the nurses but close enough to see Mimi. She looked so vulnerable with the oxygen mask on her face, that it broke my heart. I got comfortable in my chair and we waved goodnight, blowing kisses to each other. How life comes full circle, here I was taking care of her, when forty-five years earlier she had been taking care of me.

The next day when I asked the head nurse exactly what the prognosis was for Mimi, she wanted to know my relationship to her. I was trying to be tough, but with the words, "she is like my mother" I began to cry. I hated not being able to control my emotions. She began to explain how Mimi's intestines weren't doing well and that there was a large section not getting any oxygen. Hello? That is not a good thing. Why hasn't anyone just spelled it out for us? So I asked her straight out. Is she dying? She basically said yes without saying yes. My instincts were correct, now how do I tell the rest of the family?

The morning after I spoke with the nurse, the doctors came in and looked at each other saying that Mimi was doing much better. I was standing there listening to the doctors thinking, *are you kidding me? You should have seen her during the night gasping for air. Have you seen her bed sore? What about her intestines?* In front of Mimi, I just smiled and said how great that news was, kissed her, and then followed them out. Once out of earshot, I expressed my thoughts. I could not play this emotional game. She did not look better. Mimi was one of those people, who when she saw a doctor in a white coat, it was like she was looking at God. She would smile and even flirt. I explained how they were only seeing a snapshot of her and although we didn't want to lose her, we all needed to know what to expect. They beat around the bush and said that the nurse was not at liberty to say but that she was basically dying... and...... blah blah blah blah was all I heard. It was quite clear to me, I could see her health declining before my very eyes. It had been days of Mimi consistently going downhill. There were more tests, and scans of her heart to rule out congestive heart failure. They didn't find anything wrong with her heart, but they didn't have any concrete answers for us either...

My routine was the same. I would wake up and be so happy to see Mimi. I would help her, talk quietly or just sit by her side holding her hand. The days passed and even though Mimi was suffering, she had a great attitude. She still never talked about dying. I just wanted to be with her. I was in denial and wanted Mimi to live forever. We all spent the next few weeks visiting and making sure Mimi was never alone. I slept there every night, some days I never left at all. The staff couldn't believe how much support Mimi had, and how good her kids were to her. Mimi was an unbelievable woman, we would never have left her alone. The girls all came to visit her a few times. Sydney, who would never sing for anyone even though she has a beautiful voice, sang "Silent Night" for Mimi. It was so beautiful that it made me cry.

As the weeks passed Mimi's pain was getting worse. She slept most of the time because of the morphine. She couldn't get out of bed anymore, and her bedsore was horrific. As more days passed she was totally sedated and had finally stopped moaning. Seeing Mimi lying in her bed, knowing the end was near was killing me. When everyone left, I would pull my chair close to the head of her bed, get on my knees so I could put my head on the pillow next to hers and smell her hair. She always smelled like Mimi, clean and fresh, even after these weeks in the hospital. I held her hand and thanked her for everything she did for me. I told her over and over how much I loved and adored her. I asked her not to worry, told her that I would be strong, even though I would miss her so much. I asked her to watch over me and take care of all of us. Her breathing would change as if to let me know she could hear me.

Christmas was so close, I told her to let go and be free of all of this pain, yet in my heart I didn't want this to end. I selfishly wanted to have her here, even if it was just in body; I needed to have this time. I cherished those nights alone with her. The hospital was so quiet. Patients were sleeping, and I would just lie with her until I was too tired. I stayed close letting her know I was right there, that I wouldn't leave her until she was ready to go.

During the night Mimi's breathing had changed. I told her it was okay to let go and that she would be in a better place. Christmas Eve morning arrived bringing the end closer. Her breaths were so different now. She would take one big breath and then seem to hold it for the longest time. I would hold my own breath, every time. Then she would exhale. I wished her a Merry Christmas while gently washing her face with a warm cloth. Mimi actually smiled for me. I cried, I knew this was it. I knew the end was coming fast and I felt panicked. I continued to wash her face because she seemed to be comforted by this. I had called the doctor, he told me it could be minutes or hours longer, there was no way of knowing for sure.

Timothy walked in and I burst into tears as he held me in his arms. A few minutes later David and Peter walked into the room. I told them what had been happening. Within ten minutes of their arrival, as they were talking, Mimi's breathing changed again. I was watching Mimi intently. Timothy was behind me holding my shoulders. She took a big breath in… I waited for her to exhale, but it wasn't happening. I squeezed Timothy's hand. David and Peter hadn't noticed yet, but when they saw the look on my face they stopped talking. I put my head on her chest, it wasn't moving. Timothy pulled me back and held me in his arms. All the nurses came into the room. One nurse checked Mimi's pulse, giving the sign that Mimi was gone. I thought I was going to collapse, Timothy held me in his arms, as I sobbed uncontrollably. It couldn't be. Mimi. My Mimi, she was gone. How was I going to survive?

Even though I had lost both my parents and some friends, I never felt like this. This was horrific and unbearable. My heart had been ripped out. The pain was more than I could bear. I just kept looking at Mimi in disbelief, I couldn't believe that she would no longer be a physical part of my life. I wanted to stay in the room as long as I could but the nurses needed a few moments with her so we had to leave the room. I was very impatient as we all waited in the hallway. I knew I had to give David and Peter their time alone with Mimi, so I went in for a few minutes and then left again.

We were all in the room, when Shirley walked in smiling until she saw all of us. She looked at Mimi, who looked the same as she did for the past week, except without the oxygen mask. She looked at all of us. We couldn't speak, we all just started to cry, shaking our heads. Shirley walked over to Mimi and burst into tears, saying "Maw, no maw," she too was devastated. I wanted to lie down with Mimi, I definitely did not want to leave. I couldn't bare the thought of leaving her alone. The head nurse gave us a few hours and then told us we had to leave her, so they could go through the necessary next steps. I began to sob again. I could not leave her here alone. She would be alone! No way! I wanted to kick and scream like a child would. Then it hit me and something jolted me to get it together. It was Christmas Eve. Samantha, and Sidney were home waiting for me before they went to their grandparents. Monica, Kelsey, Jasmine, Kendall, and T.J., had to be told. Helen was still at work and didn't know yet either. I did not want anyone calling Helen, we all agreed that she needed to hear the news in person. Timothy and I decided we would go tell her after we went home to the girls. Samantha and Sydney wanted to stay with me but I told them not to, that I would be okay. They should be with their dad and grandparents, because I felt it was the right thing to do. I knew Mimi wouldn't want them sitting around crying with me. I would never want that in my death either.

As I write this my light just flickered. Mimi is with me. Mimi is my angel. She was in life and has been in death. Maybe I am more in tune or not afraid, but I can certainly feel Mimi's presence at times. When I feel her, I talk to her. I can smell her as if she is in the room. Sometimes when I am sleeping I can feel a presence, the room gets really cold and I can feel someone pulling the covers up to keep me warm. I am comforted to know Mimi is around me in spirit.

For Timothy and I this had been a very tough year. January through December we lost three of the most important people in our lives. Talk about a potential to destroy any individual, let alone a new marriage. Again, nothing was easy, but we did our best to support each other. While he was grieving I helped him and supported him as much as I could. I took on all the house responsibilities that we had shared and once things started to get back to normal, Mimi got sick. Then the roles reversed, except Timothy was still grieving. Mimi's illness and then death just brought it all back for him. We were at the same hospital with his dad just eleven months prior. So while I was falling apart, Timothy was trying to support me as best he could, but this was a very difficult time for sure. The expression, "Love Conquers All", holds true. We had each other and the kids to help us. Once again – "What Doesn't Kill You Makes You Stronger."

As the months and now years have gone by, I feel as if a part of me is missing. In the beginning the pain was unbearable, but with each passing year the pain subsides. I will always miss My Mimi. She will always be a part of me. I still cry, wishing I could go visit her, talk to her, and hug her, but I am comforted knowing she is watching over me.

Mothers and Daughters

BEING A MOM HAS CHANGED me as a person. My daughters have made me want to be the best version of myself. That may sound corny but it's the truth. I want them to be proud of me, and my accomplishments. I want to show them how anything is possible. I want them to have the courage and the strength to handle anything life throws at them. As a mother I have always wanted my daughters to have everything.

Through the years I have wanted to protect them from pain and sorrow. It became abundantly clear, that this would not be possible. As I have already experienced, life's journey is filled with lessons that are meant to be in our path, to teach us, and to help us evolve. My daughters would also have to have some painful experiences. My role has been to love them unconditionally, and to continue to support them as much as possible, through these experiences.

I'm not an expert in the field of depression or anxiety, but I have seen what it can do. I have known many teens and adults who suffer from anxiety and/or depression. It changes people. Growing up there were times I may have felt depressed. I can remember the feeling of dread when my alarm would go off, or crying for hours and hours for consecutive days, or weeks. Nonetheless I was always able to have fun, be with friends, and distract myself. In my mind, life had not been easy but I always had this deep desire to just be happy, and have fun. So when I could, that's exactly what I did. With any difficult time, that's how I got through it. There were also times when something in me disconnected, and I became detached in order to cope. For some people fighting these depressing feelings are impossible due to a chemical imbalance. I was fortunate enough to not be dealing with an imbalance and therefore, at certain times it may have been easier for me to cope.

What I learned watching both of my daughters, is how depression can completely change someone. Sometimes medication is needed and it's important for anyone suffering not to feel ashamed or embarrassed. Samantha had a very difficult time emotionally for many years throughout elementary school. She is a very loving, caring, sensitive young woman. Samantha always had unexplainable fears and had trouble with friends over the years. Girls were mean to her. So many times Samantha cried in my arms so hurt, and all I could do was hold her reminding her how amazing she was. High school was even worse. Samantha had one too many concussions from playing hockey. This may have played a roll, but girlfriends were still being mean. She would come home almost every day in tears. Something in Samantha was changing. It was frightening for me to watch. Logical thoughts were becoming impossible. I was unable to differentiate between her perception of the events and the actual events of her day. Every night I had to lie down with Samantha as she cried herself to sleep. Sometimes it was because her friends were being cruel, other times she was just sad, and could not explain it. It was heart breaking, and I felt lost. She was too young to be on medication, and I had heard terrible stories about teens on anti-depressants, so I just kept trying to support her.

As high school was coming to an end, her issues with friends continued, and at this point Samantha was crying every night at dinner, and still every night at bedtime. She tried speaking with psychologists but nothing was helping. When the kids were all together, Samantha would be the entertainment. She would sit under the table as if in some sort of trance, and sing a song to make everyone laugh. The first time this happened it was funny, until I saw how quickly her mood would change. Ten minutes later Samantha would be in tears. I was beginning to get very nervous. I continued to support Samantha as best I could. One of the last days of school, and six months before Mimi died, Samantha and Sydney's grandmother passed away suddenly. They were both devastated, but at least I knew why they were sad. They both seemed like they were handling their shock, and sadness.

Sydney left for a school trip to Europe and because she never had a problem leaving me, I wasn't at all worried about her. That is, until she called the first time in complete hysterics. Of course, it made sense. Sydney was so far away, her grandmother had passed away unexpectedly, and she was terrified that something was going to happen to me. It was a very long ten days for both of us, and there wasn't anything I could do to protect her from her pain.

Samantha was only getting worse. She was still crying every day and stuck to me quite a bit, but that was not very different from any other time in her life so far. Since she was little, Samantha suffered from separation anxiety and anytime I left even for a weekend, she would cry for days prior and while I was gone. December came around and Mimi was in the hospital. I knew this would only mean that Samantha would crash even further. I also knew that I would have nothing to give once Mimi was gone. I made an appointment with our family doctor, and that was when it was decided Samantha would start medication.

Despite the death of Mimi and how I was feeling, Samantha seemed to be better. That is, until almost a year later. Timothy and I were leaving for a trip to Florida and about a week before, Samantha got sick with bronchitis. By the time we left she was much better, but had to go for a check up while we were away. The day before Timothy and I were flying home Samantha called and she did not sound good at all. She said that the bronchitis had cleared but we had to go back to the doctor when

Timothy and I got home. I was holding my breath but didn't know why. It didn't make sense that we would have to go back if her bronchitis was cleared. Then Samantha told me the real reason. She began to cry and asked me not to be mad, but that she had started to cut herself. My heart broke. I reassured her that I would never be mad and that I loved her so much. I knew I couldn't ask why she did it. I had heard about kids cutting themselves, but never thought I would experience it with my own kids. I kept it together while I was on the phone, I felt so helpless and scared. She was with Sydney and Kendall and they reassured me all was fine. To me it was anything but fine. I was worried about how this was affecting the girls and I didn't want them alone with Samantha. I wanted to be on a plane that second. I could not wait to get home, all I did was cry from the moment I hung up the phone until I got home. I felt sick with worry.

Once I arrived home, I could see the deep sadness in Samantha's eyes. We went to the doctor who wasn't sure which medication to put her on. We could not get in to see any psychiatrist and Samantha kept saying she was better now that I was home. I could see that she was not. That evening as she laid her head on my lap, I could feel the sadness emanating from her. She kept insisting she was okay. Then she asked if she could go take a shower. I didn't think anything of it. Again I asked if she needed me, but she just wanted to have a shower. Two minutes later, I felt panic rise within me. I ran downstairs and put my ear on the door. I could hear Samantha sobbing uncontrollably. I banged on the door and tried to look under, terrified that I would find blood at her feet, but relieved that was not the case. Through her sobbing, Samantha tried to say she was okay. I ran upstairs to get Timothy, and called my psychologist, unsure as to what I should do. I ran back down and as I was about to call out to Samantha, I heard the clinking of scissors on the back of the toilet. I felt sick and begged for her to open the door. When she did, I broke down. The look in her eyes and on her face was unbearable. My Samantha wasn't there. With tears streaming down her face, and through her sobs she asked us what was wrong with her.

Timothy and I both held her in our arms and told her that she had no control, that it was not her fault, and that we would help her. I helped her get dressed not leaving her alone for one second. After she cut herself, it released the emotional pain, and she began to calm down.

I called her dad and we went straight to the hospital emergency upon the advice of my psychologist. Sad to say, they did not help us at all. I thank God every day that we were there to support Samantha. The intern asked Samantha every question in the book. At one point she even looked at him and said, "I know you are trying to figure out if I am bi-polar or suicidal". She reassured them that she didn't want to die, she just felt overcome by pain and sadness. She felt that cutting herself was the only way she knew how to get any relief. As a mother I was terrified that she would become suicidal at any moment.

The best help we received was from our family doctor. He saw us the very next day. I had done some of my own research and from what I read I wanted to ask about a medication that only affected the serotonin levels. That seemed like a better fit for Samantha. Although we couldn't get in to see a psychiatrist, our doctor was able to have a phone consultation in which the psychiatrist agreed that the medication needed to be changed. The process would take some time because she would have to wean off one and begin the other. Samantha was not to be left alone for the next two to four weeks.

I am thrilled to say that three years later, Samantha is still on the medication, very happy and stable. Samantha is beautiful, loving, and so giving of herself. I am so proud of her courage and strength through all of this. In sharing this story, we hope that if you feel this way, or know someone who is suffering, to please find the right help.

Through all of this and for many years Sydney felt neglected. I had tried hard over time to plan special days with Sydney. Sometimes I would even let her miss school and call it a "mental health day" so we could have mother/ daughter time. We love movies, so we usually had lunch and movie dates together. But that didn't seem to stop Sydney from feeling less important. Sydney often kept to herself and had a difficult time opening up about how she was feeling. Maybe part of her didn't want to cause problems.

There were times when Sydney had her own scary health issues as well. During a routine check up, at the doctor, he felt a lump on Sydney's abdomen. He sent us for an ultrasound and did some blood tests, which showed some elevated hormones. The doctors were concerned, and one made the mistake of mentioning that sometimes it could be an indication of a pituitary tumor. Of course, any time the word tumor is mentioned, panic sets in. It was months of worry for all of us, waiting for an MRI, and then waiting for results. Thank God they didn't find anything, but they still couldn't explain the elevated hormones. We were told not to worry.

A year later, the doctor wanted to test the levels again, to find them still elevated. Once again we were concerned. More tests were done, and we were on another emotional roller coaster. We saw a different specialist, who then told us the doctors were wrong to jump to any conclusion, and that sometime hormones can be elevated. Needless to say Sydney and I felt extremely frustrated for all the stress that had been caused.

Since Samantha had so many emotional issues, it did take a great deal of my time and energy. Three years ago, with Kendall's help, Sydney finally opened up about feeling neglected. The conversation began at 9:00 pm one night and ended at 3:00 am the following morning. There were many tears, and I was getting pretty frustrated. At times I was raising my voice out of frustration due to the fact that Kendall was speaking in code to try to help Sydney express how she felt. Sydney was not speaking, nor was she expressing whatever it was she had been keeping in for so long. Finally Sydney handed me a speech that a character from a television show had given, which resonated with her. "I spent a lot of time alone. There was a lot of benign neglect. It's not that they didn't love me. It's just that I didn't ask for much. I don't think I really knew how, and the less that I would ask for the less time that they had for me. They were just very, very involved in their own lives and into each other. I was really lost".

I burst into tears. I felt like a failure as a mother. Then I felt hurt, thinking of all the times I did go out of my way to try to help Sydney and make sure she didn't feel neglected. I then realized, that I am the adult. It wasn't about me, and what I may or may not have done. It was about Sydney, and these were her feelings. I held her in my arms, told her I was sorry, and reminded her how much I loved her. I knew it couldn't change anything. I also shared the many times I would go into her room and try to talk to her, but Sydney would keep to herself. She would close herself in. This was how Sydney coped. It was clear over the years that Sydney was angry with Samantha, which was normal for any child if they felt as though one sibling got all of the attention. It was also necessary for Samantha and Sydney to share and talk. Samantha apologized, expressing how she never meant to take anything away from Sydney. Although this was an extremely emotional evening, something good came out of it. We became even more connected as a family.

About two years ago, Sydney cried in my arms telling me that she felt depressed and needed help. I was relieved in a way, because I could sense that Sydney was not happy. I felt helpless. Any time I asked if she needed to talk, Sydney would say she was fine. I was glad to at least be able to help in some way. I found a clinic nearby where they help teens. Sydney was very private about the extent of her depression, and kept to herself about it. She was placed on medication after her first visit to the clinic, but only used it for a few months. Sydney did not want to be dependent on it, and disliked the fact that when she did feel happy – it seemed spurious.

During this time, there was a day when Samantha and Sydney returned from dinner at their dad's, and Sydney arrived in a fit of anger. I did not know what had happened. She was infuriated at a homophobic conversation that had transpired over dinner. As I was listening, I shared her anger, but to a lesser degree. Once she calmed down, she told Samantha and I that there was something she needed to tell us. I was scared, but I was so relieved when I heard her say, "I am bisexual". I looked at her and hugged her and said, "That's it? Well that is good for you, more options"! With my words, I could sense her relief. With that she began to cry really hard, I held her in my arms and both Samantha and I told her that we loved her no matter what. For Sydney, having heard horror stories of parents disowning their kids, she was afraid. I wondered how she could ever think I would judge her in any way.

I am so very proud of Sydney. She is a strong, loving, smart, wonderful, and beautiful young woman. At nineteen, she followed her heart and her dream and without even knowing how we would pay for it, decided to move to Alberta to attend a university away from home. In Canada, moving away for university is not always something students do. Sydney knew she wanted to have a fresh start and was compelled to move away. She is living her dream, and although I miss her very much, I know it is her life to live. She will always be my daughter and no distance will ever change that.

Sydney hopes that by sharing her story, any parent dealing with a child who is gay, or bisexual, will find it in their hearts, to embrace their child regardless of their sexual orientation. Everyone deserves to be loved and accepted for who they are.

I am so fortunate to have two wonderful, healthy, loving daughters. I have worked hard to be close with them, always trying my best despite my shortcomings. I have always been as open as possible with them, communicating as best I could. Obviously, when they were younger there were certain subjects that I did not talk about; that is, until then one time I was provoked.

One weekend when the girls were about ten and twelve, they went to visit their aunt with their dad, his girlfriend, their grandparents, my sister, and my nieces. Once they got home, I noticed that the girls were in a bit of a strange mood. Finally, the question was asked, "mom, do you do drugs"? I was driving at the time and almost slammed on the breaks. I was shocked and asked why they would think that. They were told that although they might think I was a great mother, there were things they didn't know about me. I was bewildered. I knew there were often negative things said about me, because this wasn't the first time my daughters returned with questions. Usually it was something they had overheard, but this time, it was something told to them directly.

Then I received a phone message from their dad's girlfriend. I was fuming when I heard her say, "you think you are such a wonderful mother, but I know who you really are. I bet you never told the girls about your affair," she rambled on and on. I ended up feeling bad for this woman once I discovered she was dealing with some mental health issues, but that didn't give her the right to attack me.

I was not going to be threatened by anyone. I had nothing to hide. I had made many mistakes in my life, but this had nothing to do with my daughters. I had no choice, but to sit them down and share the story of my affair. I was told they were too young to hear about it, but I didn't care. If anyone was trying to cause a rift in my relationship with my daughters, this had the opposite affect. They appreciated the truth and it only brought us closer together.

My Angels

I BELIEVE THERE ARE ANGELS IN all forms. Some angels are people we meet who help us through difficult times, and others come in the form of spirits. I don't remember much about my mom, but I know she has been one of my angels. She has been the presence I often felt, and the comfort when I was too afraid. My mom was my angel stopping me from hurting myself, or saving me from feeling destitute or too lonely. I have had two experiences where I literally thought I was going to die. My life flashed before me within minutes. I know in my heart there was a bigger force saving me during these moments.

Winter was just starting and it was a slightly stormy afternoon. I was in my early twenties and I never feared driving in any kind of weather. I was never a nervous driver, maybe a little impatient at times. I was driving in an area that was slightly downhill. Cars were crawling at a snail's pace, so I decided to get into the left lane and pass the cars. Suddenly, I noticed I was passing a salt truck. I looked at him and as he was waving his hand at me, I felt a chill. All of a sudden my car went completely out of control, swerving all the way left, heading straight for a tree. Nothing I was doing was helping. All of a sudden my car swerved to the right heading for another tree. Each time I swerved I was frantically trying to steer away, sometimes letting go of the steering wheel putting my hands up to my face, then the car swerved again.

After going left again and then right, side swiping a car, thinking I must have just killed someone, my car began to pick up speed and I was heading straight for a cement median. THIS WAS IT! I was done, I was sure of it. I was pumping my brakes but I was not slowing down, so I brought my hands up and I held my breath. All of a sudden my car stopped. Just stopped. It was literally a hair from hitting the cement median. I was shaking from head to toe. I could not believe my eyes when I got out to see how close I was to the median. I had to deal with the poor guy and his car that I sideswiped. He was freaking out because "his old man was going to kill him", and I felt so bad. At least he was okay. I was happy to be alive. I thought my car was dead, but I got in and it started without a problem.

I had a second experience in a car about fifteen years later, when driving with my husband John. It was another very snowy night. I knew we should not be driving, and I had a bad feeling. Sure enough, on the highway, our minivan went out of control. We were swerving back and forth, passing cars, not hitting any. The car actually did a 360 and all I remember was saying, "oh God please help us" over and over again. Then the van hit the median head on bouncing off of it, did another 360 and then suddenly we were back in the left lane going straight. What the hell? How did we not kill anyone or end up dead ourselves? I knew that for a second time there was something I could not see, helping me and saving my life.

There have been times when I'm sleeping and I feel a presence. I would get cold and, as hard as I tried, I couldn't move or open my eyes. Part of me was scared, not wanting to move, but another part of me would try to get out of bed to see who was there. I knew it was my mom and I wanted to go find her. There was always a voice, usually a deep voice with a message. One of these times, I was given someone's name, and was told to tell this person to be careful. Trust me, I was freaked out. The person I called was very intrigued. She believed in the after-life and thanked me for warning her. Oddly enough, that night was Halloween, she said she had a moment when she almost stepped off the sidewalk, then she remembered my warning. As she paused, a car whipped around the corner faster than it should have. She called me the next day to thank me.

Five months after Mimi passed away, Timothy and I had the opportunity to meet a well-known psychic, Angelina. This was very exciting for me since I had always watched the television show "Psychy" which was based on her real life experiences. As she was signing my book, I asked her how she picked whom she would communicate with. She explained that as she hears things, it's the loudest person that comes through. I wasn't sure what I was expecting or why I thought Mimi would come through, but she didn't. The experience was still very enlightening.

A year later, I had a phone consultation with Angelina, which was an incredible experience. She didn't know anything about my history. I did both a psychic reading as well as a medium reading. Angelina predicted things about my life that have come true. She saw specific things about my work as a massage therapist and how she saw me in my own office, setting products up on shelves. At that time I was renting out a room and didn't have any intention of setting anything up on shelves. Sure enough two years later, there I was setting up a new office and putting products on shelves. I had taken notes during this call, but had put them away. It wasn't something I lived by, but when I looked back and read the notes I was shocked. Angelina also saw me in another business where I would be the "ring leader", run by high-energy people. She saw this as something that was inspiring and true to my vision.

She also saw me writing a book. At the time, my book was a just thought and although I was eager to begin, I wasn't sure what the subject matter would be. Angelina said that I would be writing a book to help many people, but only in a few years. When she said it was to help people, for the longest time, I assumed I was meant to write a short cookbook on how I started living gluten free. Many people have come to me over the years expressing how daunting and overwhelming it is to become gluten-free. As time has passed, more and more books about gluten-free living had become available, and I didn't see the point in writing one of my own. Then my book began to evolve into something quite different, into sharing my story.

The second part was the Medium consultation, where Angelina connects with the dead. I knew she could do it, I knew she had done it. I read her books, I saw her live, and I needed to know Mimi and my mom were around. As for my dad, I wasn't sure I even wanted to bring him through.

The experience was unbelievable. Before we began, Angelina explained to me that she acts as the "secretary" giving me the messages that my loved ones were giving to her. First I had the opportunity to hear things about Mimi, things Angelina could never know. I hadn't yet mentioned that mom had already passed away. As she brought Mimi through, Angelina said that the first person who greeted Mimi in heaven was my mom. She described Mimi in one of her housedresses. Mimi always wore those around the house. Angelina had explained how when people move on they show themselves in a form from when they were very happy. For Mimi, she was shown to Angelina at a much younger age, vibrant and free of pain. That made me happy. "She wasn't happy with how she died, but she is happy now. She is showing me a chain around your neck, a silver key and says she is very proud of you". This didn't mean anything to me until a few years later when I received a key on a chain as part of a new business.

Angelina then brought mom through. She said how sorry my mom was for leaving me. This was something that I had to come to terms with years before. Knowing that my mom hadn't really fought to live had made me angry. I had to make the choice to forgive her, and realized that it was her journey on earth, which was meant to be for a shorter time. Also, it was something I was also meant to experience. "Your mom is showing me these little cookies, did she used to bake these for you"? I didn't remember, but I hoped she did. Angelina explained that now my mom was further away, but has always watched over me.

When I decided to give her my dad's birth date, I could hear Angelina's breathing change and she began to speak in a more cautious tone. "It's very dark, I see him with you. He is very sorry. He never meant to hurt you." Angelina took another deep breath and said, "It is very dark, there's a lot of anger, sadness, and it's very dark and very heavy. I see your dad drinking, he is an alcoholic, he is very sorry. He knows he gave you a rough start to your life. He didn't always know what he was doing; he didn't want to hurt you. He should have listened to you. He keeps apologizing".

Angelina kept relaying messages from my dad but she didn't know what I knew and what I didn't know. She thought that maybe it was too much for me to handle, and asked if I was okay. Although tears were streaming down my face, I had another odd sense of relief. At least, I got the apology I had always wanted. I feel as a Medium, this gift comes with a heavy burden and I appreciated Angelina's insight into my past and future.

The Body, Mind, and Soul

OVER THE YEARS I HAVE seen many psychologists, and experienced many forms of treatments. I have a strong belief that negative emotional experiences can manifest into physical problems. I know that many of my symptoms and physical ailments stem from my childhood. I have worked hard to be as healthy as possible, never dwelling on a diagnosis, or some unpleasant symptom. I have always exercised, and learned to have healthier eating habits. I believe in letting go of the past, but I also realize that all the talking in the world can't release certain deep-rooted emotions from traumatic experiences. Some of these emotions lay dormant on a subconscious level. As years have passed, one thing still plagues me. It is very deep-rooted and I continue to work on this. I have seen many therapists and practiced many affirmations but this feeling of not being pretty enough, thin enough, and fit enough, are like impressions on my soul.

I am always open to meeting new, gifted therapists and learning about their modalities. Donnie and I had met ten years ago in 2004 through a good friend. We met again more recently. I believe there is always a reason when certain people come into my path. When Donnie told me that she had become a certified therapist and was practicing EFT (Emotional Freedom Technique), I immediately knew why we were meeting again. I felt that I needed to experience this type of treatment.

EFT is also referred to as "tapping". It's a powerful tool that can improve your life on many levels. Many people have found it effective in helping with issues, such as anxiety, chronic pain, fears, addictions, weight control, phobias, stress and more.

This is a method that is fast and easy and doesn't require months and months of sessions. EFT is based on the principles of both ancient acupressure and modern psychology, stimulating specific meridian energy points and focusing on clearing negative emotions or physical sensations. Combined with spoken words, tapping helps calm the nervous system to restore balance or energy in the body and help reprogram the brain to respond in healthy ways. It has often been described as emotional acupuncture.

With Donnie's guidance, I began using the technique of tapping while she spoke. My intention was to release negative feelings about the sexual abuse. I felt that this would be an extra attempt to release as much as I could on a conscious level. As we went through the tapping exercise, I could feel a sense of calm but also a sense of unease. I couldn't explain it. I felt heaviness on my chest and once again it felt like something was trying to erupt from my throat. I couldn't identify my emotions. With Donnie's calming voice and as we said the words, "I choose now to release all that does not serve me, I choose now, to love and honor me," I had another epiphany. I had made the connection. I felt myself becoming more emotional, and as I began to cry and release this, I was able to identify something that seemed as though it should have been obvious to me. Through my tears, I expressed how it had been a very negative experience for me to be pretty, or attractive. It brought me negative attention from my dad and many other men in my life. I didn't have a weight problem, but always thought I did. If I did lose weight, some women would call me a bitch for no reason. It had always been very difficult for me to say anything positive about my physical body. I spent many years putting myself down. All I had done my whole life is look in a mirror to find every single flaw I could. I knew I had to create more positive thoughts about myself.

Having read "The Secret" years ago, I was compelled to read it again and also watch the movie. It's extremely powerful to watch, and a useful tool in helping to understand the power of The Law of Attraction. Our thoughts create our experiences. You may not realize that your thoughts could be stopping you from attaining what you desire. As I watched "The Secret", I was reminded of the importance of positive thoughts in every aspect of life.

A good friend recommended the book "Many Masters, Many Lives". In my opinion, past lives have a big impact on this life. This book is amazing, even if you don't believe in past lives; it may give you something to think about. This book encompasses everything I have felt and believed over the years. It confirms my belief that we are here on earth for a purpose, and that our past lives may be affecting this life. It has enhanced my own intuitive thoughts and strengthened my trust in the Universe.

Another book which has melded all of this together for me is, "The Lifeboard: Follow Your Vision- Realize Your Dreams". While learning to keep a journal of your positive thoughts and affirmations, this book will give you the tools to create your own Lifeboard. For me this was the next important step while practicing The Law of Attraction. Combining The Law of Attraction with the creation of a Lifeboard or vision board is a very powerful experience in helping you achieve your heart's desires and life goals.

Visualizing and learning how to reframe your thoughts, or the way you see a situation, is almost like changing the frame on a picture. The Universe can help all of you achieve what you want: Life goals, better health, or a happier state of mind. Learning to visualize these positive things are all key factors in co-creating a more fulfilled life.

Anne-Marie's approach encompasses all of this, and over the years these sessions have been an integral part of my personal evolution and healing. As Anne-Marie has evolved, so has her practice. During the past year she has helped me immensely by working with Quantum Reframing and coaching. Anne-Marie's Quantum Reframing and coaching techniques can help us achieve the goals we set out to accomplish in this lifetime. This is achieved by releasing the emotions that may be causing a blockage. This approach enabled me to access my own inner wisdom, by enhancing my capacity to be more conscious of my own essence. On this energetic level, Anne-Marie facilitates the release of negative emotions and beliefs, which may be getting in the way. Templates are removed and pathways are developed, allowing access to the truth within my essence. Some of these blockages were hindering my soul's progression, making it more difficult for me to reach my personal goals.

We all have a purpose on earth. Have you ever felt that you know what you need to do and yet you feel as though something is holding you back? Do you ever feel as though you're trying so hard to reach a goal and yet no matter what, it's not happening for you? It's almost like wanting to start an exercise program but an old hip injury is preventing you from starting. First you would need to get help to heal the injury. You may see a massage therapist, osteopath or physiotherapist. Those modalities can help your body access its own ability to heal the injury. An increase in the mobility in your hip, allows you to move more freely, and therefore achieve your exercise goals.

There could also be emotions in this life that may be creating a blockage in part of your body. Many emotions, conscious or subconscious, can have an undesirable impact on the physical body. This can create blockages, therefore no matter how hard you try to fix aches and pains, something far deeper stops the healing from taking place. By uncovering the emotion and where it is stored in my body, Anne-Marie helps me release it on an energetic level. Once it's revealed and the charge removed on the energetic level, this sets the body on the path for self-healing.

The most recent session helped me understand my emotions and experiences on a much deeper level than ever before. I truly believe that I am at the time in my life where I am ready to release more and share my experiences in order to help others. Knowing all that I want to accomplish, things from the past needed to be brought to the surface and resolved.

Anne-Marie can identify the negative emotions that may come from childhood, a past experience, event, cultural, inherited, or even a past life. Emotions and stress can create an imbalance in the body. Restoring this balance is a key factor in creating a healthier, and more meaningful life.

Anne-Marie clearly saw emotions of frustration and anger within me, creating blockages in my intestines. During these sessions, she acts as the messenger, and is guided by my own inner wisdom. Anne-Marie helped to me understand more deeply that being sexually abused and violated for so many years, created a great deal of negativity in my subconscious.

How could I trust the adults, or my own parents? Why wasn't anyone protecting me? How could I trust myself since I couldn't stop these things from happening? I was being treated in a sexual way without asking for it. People's perceptions that I had asked for the abuse, also lead me to feel so frustrated and angry. Why couldn't people understand and support me? My friendly, fun loving ways, or being attractive had become such a negative thing. How could I ever look in the mirror and see someone attractive? My subconscious felt it was bad to be attractive. Any attention on a sexual level brought negativity. Even though I was not consciously aware of these thoughts, this was clear to Anne-Marie while she was working with me.

Many people fear emotions from childhood, keeping them hidden away and pretending they don't exist. This may be easier, but unfortunately there can be a physical impact from unresolved, negative emotional experiences. Past experiences shape who we are, and how we react to situations and function in our everyday lives. Healing from the past is a very key component to being the best you can be.

As I have evolved, I realize that the most important thing is inner beauty, and knowing I am a good person. Everything else is perception. We are loved for who we are not what we look like. Many of you may struggle with this; I know that I am not alone. I continue to struggle with this, because changing a thought pattern, that has been constant for over forty years can be difficult. I will never give up and every day I make a point to say one positive thing about my physical self. As years have past and through different treatments I am proud of the changes I have made, and I continue to embrace my journey of self-empowerment.

The Universe at Work

ALTHOUGH CIRCUMSTANCES IN LIFE CAN be difficult, the important thing is how you react and deal with these difficulties. It is important to recognize something positive in everything that happens. Some of my past experiences were not pleasant, but those unpleasant experiences still brought something better into my life. Even though life may not always be easy, if you truly want to make changes, you can make it happen.

I was enjoying my career as a massage therapist and had built a good business for myself. Yet, somehow there never seemed to be enough money. Timothy and I always had to use a line of credit for vacations, even though we have never been extravagant. We rarely eat in restaurants, and I don't buy jewelry, or expensive clothes and shoes. Our biggest expense has been spoiling our kids while on vacations. In opening myself up to wanting an even better life, so many good things, opportunities, and people have come into my path.

One day out of the blue, my friend Tasha called me to tell me that she had a business opportunity for me. This one phone call has changed my life in so many ways. Tasha had started her own business in Network Marketing and wanted to expand her business. The concept of Network Marketing made sense to me, since it was how I built my massage business. In fact it was something I was doing every day, simply by recommending protein shakes or vitamins to my clients. I was definitely giving a great deal of business to the local health food store. I was quite dismissive about the whole opportunity at first, giving Tasha all the reasons I hear from so many people; I am too busy, I have no time, I am shy, not a sales person, etc. Once I thought about it, I realized these were all just excuses. If I truly wanted to create financial freedom, I had to make a change. I also realized that this was my lottery ticket in disguise, and even though I had bet the same lottery numbers for over twenty years, I never won. If I worked hard at this, it would be like winning a lottery that keeps on giving.

Many people have a misconception about Network Marketing, usually because they really don't know what it is. In my opinion, this is an opportunity of a lifetime. It is something I can share with other people, fit it into my busy life, and build along side my massage career, writing my book, my family life, and other commitments.

The business model is very simple, but it is not always easy. It takes hard work, commitment, and time. I was willing to make the time and do the work, because I really wanted to make the changes in my life. Any change in life takes time and effort. Some of you may want change, but may not be willing to do the work to achieve the desired outcome. It's all a matter of how badly you want the changes. It's like losing weight or getting in shape. Anybody can do it, because the process is simple. Eat healthy, take in fewer calories, and burn more calories through exercise. As we all know, it takes discipline to change or create new habits. Exercising and having to cut back on the foods you love may seem like torture to some of you. If you truly want to make those changes, then you have to be willing to work hard at it, and take the time to achieve your goals.

We have all been programmed to find a job and make money for other people. Doesn't it make more sense to build a business for yourself? I love the opportunity to build my own business, while helping others become successful. Even though this may not be for everyone, in my opinion, there is nothing more rewarding than helping others make life changes, which allows them to build their own dreams. Everybody benefits from his or her own efforts and hard work. In any business and to achieve any dream, the key is to never give up.

As The Universe works for me, I see signs of support everywhere. It becomes so clear as I experience so many serendipitous encounters because of unexpected changes in my day. I always look for the meaning of the encounter and listen intently during the conversation. Over the years I began to realize how every thing in my path was put there for me to learn something. Amazing friends have been brought into my life because I now had a reason to reach out to meet new people. Some of my closest friends are in my life because of this amazing opportunity. Everything does happen for a reason and the more faith you have, and the more you believe in the life process, the stronger your instincts will be. My instincts become stronger every day.

Wealth and Emotions

ONCE I DECIDED TO MAKE big changes in my life and create ways to have financial abundance, something became very clear to me; I did not have a good relationship with money. Money was abundant during the times in my life when I was most unhappy. For years I had been rejecting abundance on a subconscious level. When I found myself living in a difficult financial situation, without realizing it my negative thoughts were creating more debt. The Law of Attraction was at work once again. For me there were different reasons why the debt had been created. Never having learned how to budget, I had always just spent money. I believe there was also a higher purpose for me to experience financial debt. I could always sympathize with others when they talked about being financially stressed, but once I experienced it myself, only then, could I truly empathize with others.

Each of you may have a different relationship with money. For some of you wealth may be important because you like to have the finer things in life, or a certain status. Others may want money to help family and donate to charities. Some of you may not care about having much money. Many of you may be afraid to have money, because of a past experience. Each of you has an experience that may be affecting how you see money and wealth. This can be traced back to childhood, watching parents deal with debt, or even bankruptcy. Without realizing it, by constantly worrying about debt or bankruptcy and focusing on how much you don't want it, you are continuously attracting exactly what you don't want. This goes back to the Law of Attraction.

Growing up, my dad was wealthy. As a kid I don't ever remember thinking much about money, how much we had or didn't have. All I knew was that I was happiest when I was with Mimi, and she did not have much money. Even now, many years later, if I mention to anyone that my dad had a condo in an affluent area in Miami, people always make the same comment, "oh you were one of those spoiled kids". The assumption is always there. I grew up with a dad who had money, I was spoiled because I had a car and I went to Florida on spring break, so supposedly life was easy. That was a misconception for many people. It created feelings of guilt for having financial abundance. The materialistic things were very much unrelated to my happiness. Long ago I learned that money did not make me happy. Happiness comes from within. It has been a long road to understanding my own relationship with money and wealth. For me wealth had a very negative association with my happiness and I was not even aware of it.

My father didn't know how to provide us with love. He only knew how to provide us with materialistic things. I don't have many memories of spending quality time with my dad, teaching me anything, having any sort of heartfelt conversations. I was always very appreciative of going to Florida on spring break, having my own car, but it didn't replace the void inside me.

At the age of 21, when my dad passed away, many things happened. My sister and I were given a large amount of money without any structure, guidance, or foundation on how to deal with it. Looking back, I realize that I basically lost my entire family over the next year, all because of money. There were fights with my cousins and lawyers, and still, money could not replace the void. Without realizing it, this created another negative emotion relating to money and wealth.

The way the Will was made, the agreements, the disbursements of the shares of the business, were set in stone. I am not complaining now, nor was I then. This did allow me a very good quality of life, eliminating the need to worry about money. I definitely knew I was very lucky to have this financial freedom at such a young age. I always appreciated having more choices and never thought that I was better than anyone. I have always been generous, even when I didn't have the means to be. I never realized people were judging me. Only years later, did I learn how many people were gossiping or assuming my life was easier because I had money.

While receiving money from my dad's estate, I had my husband take care of the investing, which in itself speaks volumes. Years later when I was on my own living with my two daughters, everything was paid for, and I remember the day I opened a statement that read $400,000.00. I felt so fortunate. My retirement was all set. I felt so blessed that I was able to be home with my kids and very happy, knowing I had the freedom of choice. I wanted to work, as my kids got older, but for now my first priority was my kids.

Fast forward a year, and the market crashed. I had many shares in BCE and Nortel. I was only reminded of this because of a serendipitous encounter while I was having lunch with my dear friend Ronni. We happened to meet a financial advisor who shared his memory of the day the markets crashed. What struck me from this conversation was what he described. He had been in Florida at the time, and he remembers people frantically making calls. When he walked out onto the beach, people were grabbing their phones and scurrying all around. As he described this, I realized that when the market crashed and I had lost a great deal of money, and I had not reacted. My statement next month was less than a quarter of what it had been the month before. Putting the statement aside, I didn't react and moved on with my day.

Many associate wealth with negativity without even realizing it. How many people see someone driving an expensive car and instinctively think how that person has money and must be a snob. There can also be feelings of jealousy. Yes there are mean rich people, but there are also many mean poor people. Some people are just miserable, but you would not look at a poor person and assume they are snobby. Yet, there is often a negative association with a rich person, or someone who is perceived as being rich. I have often heard people say, "Oh their life is easier, they have it all, they have no problems, what more could they want"?

Money in itself doesn't make someone happy. It can temporarily make you happy when buying material things, but true happiness comes from within. I have lived the life of never worrying about money and also lived the life of constantly worrying about finances. I have to say that emotionally, I was happiest in my life when I felt loved. I used to tell Timothy how frustrating it was that my life seemed to be a trade-off. I always had one or the other. I was finally in a happy marriage and we were struggling with too much debt. With those words, I realized I was putting that into The Universe. I was stating that my life was a trade-off. I decided it was time to make *both* a part of my life. I deserved to have it all! Believe me, this decision didn't happen over night. I have spent a few years stressing financially, wondering how we could change our situation. With all of these thoughts, I knew it was time to re-read The Secret and use The Law of Attraction. It is normal to get caught up with everyday life and forget that we are creating something negative in our lives.

Once you can imagine, feel and think about a life of abundant wealth, The Universe will bring you what you need to acquire that. Some people may let it pass them by, but true evolution and tapping into your own inner wisdom, will allow you to see an opportunity, even if it's in disguise. It's not something that happens quickly, since any change takes time. Now I welcome a life filled with financial abundance, freedom of choice, and the ability to help so many people. With each lesson I have learned, I know that going forward I will do things very differently. I know I will be very comfortable with financial abundance, and I will be free of caring about of any judgment.

F.E.A.R. of Failure

"I have not failed. I've just found 10,000 ways that won't work."

-Thomas Edison

YOU HAVE BEEN BORN INTO a life and you are in control of your destiny. Your soul chose this life and the experiences you are meant to live. I see this so clearly as I have evolved in my own life and lived my own experiences. Each of you has been put here on Earth to learn something unique to you. Have you ever felt as though you live the same pattern? What is the common emotion attached to that pattern? For some of you it may be to learn to trust, or to not judge, or to eliminate jealousy. And for others it can be emotions, like anger, frustration, or even fear. There are many different things you may need to learn in this life.

F.E.A.R is a paralyzing emotion that may be hindering your life, and choices. Learning to let go of this fear is crucial. Some fear is necessary, the fear that will protect you from things that can be dangerous or life threatening. The other fear, the fear of failing, not having the outcome you hoped for, the fear of not getting a job, or even the fear of success, can hinder your progression in this life. So many of you are stopping yourselves from doing something great because you are afraid of failing.

What does failing even mean? The word fail really bothers me. If you try to do something that doesn't have the desired outcome, does that mean you have failed? I often hear people talk about failure and the word burns through me. In my opinion, the only thing you can fail is a written test. Other than a written test, what really measures this "failure" everyone talks about? If you set goals and don't quite get there, some of you may look at it as failure. Imagine that you have a monthly sales goal for your business. You decide you want 10,000 in sales, but you get 8,000 instead. Have you failed? No, you made it 80 % of the way!

Feel your fear and try to determine what it is you are afraid of. Is it in fact failure? Are you afraid of what others may think of you? Or are you afraid of succeeding because you are not sure how to handle the success? Many people have a fear of success and sometimes don't even realize it, until they have the opportunity to become successful. Often these fears stem from childhood, something they experienced growing up, seeing something negative happen once a loved one acquired success. There are so many things that may have been witnessed in childhood that have a deep impact on your present life. It doesn't always have to be something traumatic, the important thing is to find the link.

Any effort and accomplishment is a success. You may *FALTER* along the way, but that is perfectly normal. A certain goal may not be achieved, but that only means that you may need a little "tweaking" in your attempt to achieve your goal. Please do not look at something as failure. Put a positive spin on everything you do, and be proud of what you have accomplished, even if you have faltered along the way. From this you will *EVOLVE,* you will learn something about yourself and about your experience. As you continue this journey and follow your heart, you will *ACHIEVE* smaller goals in the process. *REPEAT* these steps until you reach your goal. The important lesson is to never give up! If you know you have not done what needs to be done in order to achieve your goals, then set your goals again, and again.

Believe in yourself. Never give up. Know that sometimes things aren't meant to be at a certain time, be patient. Please continue your journey, believe in yourself, trust in life, and your own evolution. Continue to have faith knowing that in time you will have the life you have always dreamed of having.

"Many of life's failures are people who did not realize how close they were to success when they gave up." Thomas Edison

FALTER - EVOLVE- ACHIEVE —REPEAT

Parting Thoughts

LIFE IS A JOURNEY FILLED with lessons. I felt compelled to share my story to help and inspire you to be the best you can be. Every person goes through difficult times, some more than others. My life lessons have made it clear that we need to heal from the past, to help the small child inside all of us.

My life so far has made one thing abundantly clear: Our life experience is the best education life has to offer. Through each hardship, we learn a lesson and find our inner strength. We are truly capable of handling so much. We all have the power; it is in each and every one of us.

Throughout my experiences I have learned that people perceive things about others according to their own perceptions. The wrong perception by others of who I am has been a source of frustration for me at times. I began to realize that each person is a product of their own life circumstances, and they may be reacting to a situation based on their own personal experiences.

I have often felt judged and that has been very difficult for me. I was being judged and people were making assumptions about me, even though they had no idea what my life was like. Through this I have learned not to judge others, and feel that those who judge harshly should look in the mirror and decide if they like the reflection. Chances are there is something that makes that judgmental person very unhappy.

The need to judge those around them may be easier than changing what they don't like about themselves.

I truly feel that everything in our path is there for a reason. I have learned to stop asking why, and just accept what is, knowing that each experience has a higher purpose. I feel a sense of serenity, and calmness believing that everything we live through is meant to be. Every experience has shaped who I am as a person, mother, wife, friend, stepmother, massage therapist, business entrepreneur, and now author. For me, it is not important who I was as a person, what matters most to me now, is the person I have become.

I hope *With All My Heart*, that my words have touched you in a way that will allow you to create an even better version of yourself. As I finish this book, I am overwhelmed with emotion. I have fulfilled a dream, and completed another step in my journey. I hope that my words have resonated with you, and something I have written has inspired you to realize your own true potential.

I am filled with gratitude for the family and life I now have. I feel loved by my amazing family and my awesome friends. I look forward to every day and the wonderful experiences yet to come.

I would love to change the world into a better place, but that can be an overwhelming task. All we can really do is change ourselves a little bit at a time, and in doing so, I believe *With All My Heart*, that we can change the world. My wish for you is to live the most empowered and enlightened life.

With All My Heart,
Beth

"Life is a story that is all twists and turns. All that matters is the lessons we learn…We are all Unfinished Songs, waiting for the best part to come along. You can write the song and write the story." Celine Dion

References:

Byrne, Rhonda. *The Secret*. New York: Atria, 2006. Print.

Céline Dion. "Unfinished Songs." *Loved Me Back to Life*. Sony Music Entertainment, 2013. CD.

Shifrin-Cassidy, Sue, Linda Blum Huntington, and Eva Adrienne Anderson. *The Lifeiboard: Follow Your Vision, Realize Your Dreams* San Francisco; East Coast Girls, 2010. Print.

Tamaro, J. (Writer), & Haber, M. (Director). (2010). I'm Your BoogieMan [Television series episode]. In S. Choksey, R. Chong, & C. Griffin (Producers), Rizzoli & Isles. Los Angeles, California: Turner Network Television (TNT).

Weiss, Brian L. *Many Lives, Many Masters*, New York: Simon & Schuster, 1988. Print.

To contact Elizabeth McLennan feel free to email her at withallmyheart. em@gmail.com